WOLFE STUDIES

Also by Anthony E. Shaw

The Faithful Manager:
Using Your God Given Tools for Workplace Success
(2013)

Two Minutes with the Faithful Manager
(Alive Radio Network 2014)

WOLFE STUDIES

Essays and Critical Reviews

Anthony E. Shaw

Published by Aventine Press
55 East Emerson St.
Chula Vista CA 91911
www.aventinepress.com

ISBN: 978-1-59330-970-1

Library of Congress Control Number: 2020901454
Library of Congress Cataloging-in-Publication Data
Wolfe Studies/Anthony E. Shaw

Printed in the United States of America

Praise for *Wolfe Studies:*

"The author discusses in great detail the narrative genius of the original series, expressed in Stout's decision to make Archie's perspective the principal one, a literary strategy that, in eschewing omniscience, permits a more accurate representation of the investigatory search for the truth . . . more than just a storehouse of trivia . . . furnishes consistently incisive interpretations of both Stout's work and the attempts to re-create it . . . an impressively exhaustive account of what amounts to decades of homage to Stout's work as well as the extant literature on it."

Kirkus Reviews

Preface

Over forty years after his death, Rex Stout and his creations Nero Wolfe, Archie Goodwin, and company are still read, enjoyed, and appreciated by audiences young and once young. After 1975, the last original story, *A Family Affair*, is succeeded by the recreations of Robert Goldsborough that are sought and read by a devoted fan base. From 2000 to 2002, the A & E series *A Nero Wolfe Mystery*, achieves record high ratings for the network, and attracts a loyal following among longtime fans and newcomers. The series still sells in DVD format and is viewed consistently on You Tube. Nero Wolfe is a cultural landmark. The books, films, television and radio programs, and theatrical plays continue to entertain with no end in sight. Nero Wolfe and his world, eighty years after their introduction, are timeless.

In this book, I look at how they are portrayed, enlivened, and presented in writing and the visual media by artists interpreting Rex Stout's creations, settings, and references. Are these recreations faithful to the world Stout built and audiences have appreciated for over eight decades? Though based on in-depth research and the analysis of many and various viewpoints, the opinions that follow are solely my own.

There are several excellent compendiums of Wolfe-related information, but I've grown tired of the typical hit-and-run critiques ("It stinks," "I loved it," "not very good") of the re-creations of the Wolfe world. I believe honest criticism is absolutely necessary. Any number of dishonest critics don't have the integrity to sign their own names to their opinions – proof of intellectual poverty. My name is on what I believe. I intend to start some new arguments, maybe settle a few outstanding ones, and stimulate ever greater interest in the world of Wolfe. Let the debates begin! Enjoy.

Contents

"And I decided just to write stories and to try to make them
as good stories as I could."
- Rex Stout, Books and Authors Luncheon (1966)

"You and Rex Stout are the ones that keep me awake . . ."
- Paul Sorvino's character to Angela Lansbury's Jessica Fletcher
Murder, She Wrote, "Three Strikes, You're Out!" (May 7, 1989)

"In the immortal words of Nero Wolfe, 'Pfui!'"
- Gene Barry as Captain Amos Burke
Burke's Law, "Who Killed Cassandra Cass?"
(September 30, 1964)

Introduction: Wolfe Outside of Stout

I discovered Nero Wolfe and his world in 1966 when I was eleven years old.

In August that year, my older brother LeRoy, six years my senior, brought home a copy of *PS* magazine, and in it was an interview with Rex Stout. LeRoy, who became a lawyer, legal scholar, and law school dean, introduced me to books and the joys of reading at an early age. I bless him for it. He revered reading and higher education; he gave me access to his substantial library, ranging from Shakespeare to science fiction and much more in-between.

He did not have any Rex Stout, but the profile in *PS* led me to a tiny, below street level bookstore on Fulton Street in downtown Brooklyn, where I bought my first volume of Wolfe in 1966: *Black Orchids* in paperback for sixty cents – big money for a book in those days, at least to an eleven-year-old. I was promptly and properly hooked.

In the ensuing years I visited that shop regularly, hunting for more Wolfe when I could scrape together the money. *Fer de Lance* was my second purchase, and in July of 1969 I bought *Too Many Cooks*. I know the order in which I bought them because I penciled it in on the first page of the first fourteen books. I still have these weathered paperbacks, pages brittle and browned, covers and spines creased, worn, and shaken.

Over the course of the intervening half century, I've bought and read every Nero Wolfe story and plenty of other works by and about Rex Stout and his monumental – in all senses – creation.* Moreover, during these years I've read and re-read every story several times, on a regular cycle (or re-cycle) at two or three-year intervals.

As with my fellow Wolfe devotees, I've taken Stout, Wolfe, Goodwin, and the rest of the crew into my home and my life.

I have known my dearest personal friend since the first day of freshmen orientation at college, over forty-six years ago. I have known the Wolfe universe seven years longer – the brownstone, Fritz's cooking, the books, the words, the beer, Archie's swagger, Cramer's cigars.

Rex Stout's death in 1975 heightens the desire for more of his creations. It becomes a quest for just about anything and everything to fill the void of no more original material. The hungry but discerning reader scours the broadcast and print media for content that, at minimum, strives for Stout's well-established quality and standards. Expectations are high.

Consequently, the efforts over the years of those other than Stout to portray and then extend the Wolfean corpus arrive and invoke responses in a variety of ways, from exhilaration and thankfulness to revulsion and disdain.**

Two Nero Wolfe films are made in the 1930s, *The League of Frightened Men* (1937, directed by Herbert Biberman and written by Joseph Anthony, Howard J. Green, and Bruce Manning) and *Meet Nero Wolfe* (1936, directed by Alfred E. Green and written by Guy Endore, Eugene Solow, and Edward Chodorov), based on the novel *Fer de Lance*. ***

The world of Wolfe is translated to radio. There is a particular pleasure in listening to these spoken dramas from the 1940s, 1950s, and 1980s (the most recent broadcast from Canada), the early ones recalling an era without the dominance of television. The listener builds the drama's setting mentally, and individual imaginations are allowed to run free. To corrupt a Nero Wolfe book title, dramatize it yourself. Six actors voice Wolfe, the most famous being Sydney Greenstreet. The first three series in the 1940s and 1950s are done in a fast-paced, breathy style, common for radio programs of that time. With thirty minutes or so to fit in the whole story, dead or wasted air is not an option: speak loudly and quickly, describe what the listener can't see, and move to the conclusion. Yet, these programs are entertaining and often funny, intentionally or not. Wolfe is once introduced on air as a chair-borne mass of unpredictable intellect. Stout pronounces the radio programs during his lifetime "unbearable." The Canadian Broadcasting Corporation series in 1982 has thirteen episodes, based on adaptations of Stout's original stories. The levels of quality, production, and fidelity to the stories are significantly higher than its radio predecessors.

There are four attempts to create and sustain television shows based on Nero Wolfe. For the first attempt in 1959, *Nero Wolfe*, the executive producer is the brother of Rex Stout's friend, Clifton Fadiman. A pilot is filmed (and perhaps other unreleased episodes are also filmed), but the series is never broadcast, it being aborted for a comedy program in its place on the CBS schedule for 1959.

A parody of Nero Wolfe is presented in a 1964 television episode of *Burke's Law* – the character "Caligula Fox" is acted by Thomas Gomez.

The next effort is a made-for-television movie, also titled *Nero Wolfe*, filmed in 1977 as a pilot for a series on CBS. This film is based on the novel *The Doorbell Rang*. Next in time is the 1981 television series *Rex Stout's Nero Wolfe* on NBC. This is the regular programming of the series for which the 1977 film is the pilot. The A & E Network's *A Nero Wolfe Mystery*, airing from 2000 to 2002, is first a pilot film, then a series.

Italian, German, and Russian television each produce limited series of Nero Wolfe stories, with Italy doing it twice. Russia and Italy have particularly avid Wolfe fan bases.

Then there are the written re-creations, specifically the fourteen books over the last thirty plus years by Robert Goldsborough, a former Chicago journalist and adman, and a certified fan of the corpus.

Fortunately, there are Wolfe pastiches galore. A visit to the website of the Nero Wolfe literary society discloses numerous links to takes on Nero Wolfe, from solemn to silly. Alan Vanneman's *Three Bullets: A Nero Wolfe Threesome,* and Loren D. Estleman's creation *Nearly Nero: The Adventures of Claudius Lyon, the Man Who Would Be Wolfe* are two worthy examples. The back issues of *Ellery Queen's Mystery Magazine* contain many more, as do the archives of the literary society's publication, the *Gazette.* There are four stage productions of Nero Wolfe stories from 2009 to 2018 (the first one in Italy), including the latest one in which all the characters' genders are switched; I'm not sure how either Wolfe or Stout would take to that!

There is much insight to be gained into the background and context of the Wolfe stories and their author from the following:

> *Nero Wolfe of West Thirty-Fifth Street* by William S. Baring-Gould
>
> *Rex Stout: A Majesty's Life* by John McAleer
>
> *At Wolfe's Door* by J. Kenneth Van Dover
>
> *The Archie Goodwin Files* edited by Marvin Kaye

Stout Fellow by O. E. McBride

The Nero Wolfe Files edited by Marvin Kaye

The Nero Wolfe Cookbook by Rex Stout and the Editors of Viking Press

Rex Stout by David R. Anderson

The Nero Wolfe Handbook by Rev. Frederick G. Gotwald.

Collectively, they are valuable reading for the study and appreciation of all things Wolfe.

The foregoing is not meant to be an exhaustive review but an illustrative one. Nero Wolfe is always interesting. The public appetite for more of him remains unsatisfied. Wolfe and Goodwin are alive in our accumulated imagination. They are "ageless, invincible, and unchanging."****

Source:

John McAleer, *Rex Stout: A Majesty's Life* (2002)

*A November 29, 1986 *Philadelphia Inquirer* article quotes an estimate of 100 million Rex Stout books sold worldwide, almost all of them the Nero Wolfe series.

** The proper name for the body of Rex Stout's Nero Wolfe literary works.

*** Reasonably viewable DVD copies of both films are available from LovingtheClassics.com.

*****Sherlock Holmes in Washington,* Universal Pictures (1943)

I.
Third Eye Blind

Recently, I was upbraided online for referring to the character Nero Wolfe as "Nero." The audacity! I used the character's first name!

My measured response, if a tad snarky: Nero Wolfe is fiction, the character is not real. Even my eight-year-old son knows the difference. It's "Bugs," not "Mr. Bunny." Fiction is not wished into reality.

Perhaps what intrigues me the most about this mini tempest in a virtual teapot is the reality that the president of the United States, a person with a real title befitting the post, is often publicly called anything except the proper title: first name, a nickname, an epithet, a liar, and other things not printable in decent company. It's "the president," period, full stop. A real human being. Yet, I don't see any recognition, or any meaningful admonition about this sad leap from on-the-ground reality to fantasy. Like or dislike the person, it shouldn't be an issue—the person exists. If one desperately wants reality to be fiction, does it become so?

If life is a fantasy, then there is no compass of reality, and social standards become whatever any individual feels they should be. There is no president; the office doesn't carry a title; no one need follow the established rules or obey the social contract. Reason is usurped by emotion-driven perception and feelings overrule everything.

If fiction comes to be regarded and respected as reality, and reality takes on the habiliments of fiction, we face an unstable future. Citizens become shallow fanboys and haters, lazy extremists with no depth of logic and no dimension of reason. Their rationale is that reality doesn't matter so long as their fantasy fits their purpose. Discourse transforms into hectoring. Life loses dignity; it is no better than a circus or a cartoon. People mutate into characters; instead of showing their faces, they post images of Sherlock Holmes or Daffy Duck as identification. It can be posited that we are already on that road. Just check Facebook; there this is the norm. Life becomes "a collective hallucination" of poseurs.

Which brings us back to Nero, um, I mean Mr. Wolfe and fiction. Nero, we hardly know you. In fact, we don't really know him, the inner him, at all.

What readers do know is how the character Archie Goodwin sees him; what Archie knows, but presumably not what he doesn't know about him; what Archie has seen and experienced concerning him, but presumably not what he hasn't. In short, the reader has only an Archie-centric picture of Nero Wolfe. And Archie, for the reader's better or not-so-great fortune, only has what author Rex Stout wants Archie to have about the Great Man.

One of the enduringly fascinating elements of the Wolfe stories is Stout's decision to tell them in Archie's voice instead of an omniscient one. In the words of Robert Frost, "that has made all the difference." An omniscient storyteller, versus a first-person narrator, could never achieve the singular personal relationship displayed between Wolfe and Goodwin, nor the seriocomic elements of the narration. Archie doesn't take himself too seriously, and (sycophants, take note) he is constantly poking pins in Wolfe's sometimes inflated and often self-centered approach to fictional life. Some fictional things need to stay unknown, at the very least temporarily, to enhance the reader's sense of discovery, propelling the reader forward in the story. While an omniscient storyteller can attempt to hide or obfuscate elements, it doesn't work nearly as convincingly as it does through a single character only knowing enough of the story at certain points. If that character is as strongly drawn as Stout draws Archie, there is no substitute. Stout's biographer, John McAleer quotes the author:

"It's Archie who really carries the stories, as narrator. Whether the readers know it or not, it's Archie they really enjoy."

Moreover, what distinguishes the Wolfe stories from other, pedestrian detective fiction is that rather than just telling a story about the search for a thing – a golden platypus, as in one flimsy short story pastiche recently or a killer, for examples – these are stories about the search for reason and the truth. One person's story of the venture for the truth is far more compelling, captivating, and human than an omniscient view. One hopes the omniscient knows the truth, as we don't. A *New Yorker* profile of Stout in 1949 makes this distinction about the Wolfe stories:

"[Wolfe] solves mysteries by spotting bad logic and exposing it in choice English."

Life is me seeing you seeing me seeing you. We owe that construction to Dr. R. D. Laing, a prophet of the psyche as relevant to our appreciation of the mysteries of the mind today as Dr. Freud was a century ago. We aren't omniscient. In his work *The Divided Self,* Dr. Laing states:

"We cannot help but see the person in one way or other and place our constructions or interpretations on 'his' behavior, as soon as we are in a relationship with him."

How accurately does that describe the Wolfe-Goodwin relationship? Right on target. Archie uses his own colors to draw Wolfe for the reader's illumination.

How often in the stories does Archie admit that he has no idea what Wolfe is up to or what Wolfe really thinks about a particular subject (women's legs, for example)? Or why Wolfe does something? How many times does Wolfe engage Saul and not tell Archie what Saul is going to do?

In "Murder Is Corny," Archie is the accused; Wolfe still won't clue him in.

We're as up in the air as Archie. Isn't that ambiguity part of what makes Wolfe qua Goodwin so intriguing? As long as we are speculating, doesn't that also apply in the reverse? How Wolfe, through Goodwin, sees Goodwin (supposedly able to understand and seduce all women, for example)?

Dr. Laing would have a ball psychoanalyzing them both.

I maintain the principal reason the first three of the four American attempts to televise the Wolfe stories are less than satisfactory (much less) is that they try to tell the stories without Archie as the narrator, from a non-Archie-centric point of view. They are just more television detective stories, nothing special. Thus, they all begin from a doomed to fail starting point. There are no stories without Archie's voice. They are Archie's voice. Everything is "as seen by Archie."

Timothy Hutton succeeds as Archie in *A Nero Wolfe Mystery* because he has the voice; he's telling the story. Once the viewer believes him, it moves along nicely, credibility intact. Without him, the viewer's individual judgment takes control – not Wolfe as we expect him to be; now he is helter-skelter. The Wolfean world is an ordered universe based on what is established, expected, and required, of which the reader needs assurance of a fixed mental picture. Archie's.

There exists within each story's framework the hidden element of "What is Wolfe doing and thinking while all this is happening?" Part of Stout's genius, and he is a genius storyteller, is demonstrated in those points in the stories where Archie tells Wolfe that he (Archie) is onto him (Wolfe). Case in point: at the end of *The Silent Speaker*, Archie says he knows Wolfe found those cylinders before the staged discovery accomplished by Fritz. Reading that, one knows Archie is right because through Archie, Wolfe's theatricality is confirmed. Wolfe speaks about Archie in *The Doorbell Rang*: "he likes an audience as well as I do."

We see Wolfe through Archie's eyes and convince ourselves this is accurate. After all, doesn't Archie live with him? Think about the "relapses" Wolfe experiences in the early stories. Why do they occur? Archie guesses at their origins and tries to reverse them, but we only know what he knows – in these instances, almost nothing that informs. Eventually Wolfe recovers and the story continues. Fate? Design? Flummery?

Walt Disney and his studio, in the early 1930s, at the same time as the first Wolfe book is written, develop a theory of how to attract and attach the interest of audiences in fictional characters. Disney believes that through what he labels "personality," a unique set of characteristics that "coalesce(d) to define" the creation, a character elicits a purely emotional and bonding response from the viewer or reader. Moreover, the theory proposes this is achievable through "plausible impossibility," the extraordinary traits that audiences will nevertheless believe in the characters.

In the case of Wolfe's character, these features include:

- He never ages.

- He survives and thrives without much human physical interaction.
- He is obese without suffering diabetes, heart disease, or other medical consequences.
- He consumes gallons of beer with no effects of alcoholism or liver disease.
- He is acclaimed the greatest detective, though grudgingly by some.

One observer describes him as:

". . . shrewd, lazy, acute, authoritative, childish, long-winded, selfish, bulimic, cynical, snobbish, and sometimes unbearable."

Above all the foregoing, he is perfectly content with his life – eating, drinking beer, tending his orchids, reading extensively, and using his energies sparingly. Rex Stout's Nero Wolfe achieves the effect of personality through the author's meticulous skill with words and descriptions. Critic Benjamin Welton observes, "Much of the charm of these novels is the result of Mr. Stout's craftsmanship . . . his novels bristle with sharp dialogue and a leisurely view of life."*

Wolfe and Archie are special. Special fictional characters, not hallucinations. I enjoy them and have for more than half a century. If I don't treat them as living, breathing people, that's me. If I'm going to hero-worship, it must be a human being, not a concept or a figment or a set of words on a page. Someone in the flesh, living or departed, whom I see, perhaps seeing people like me, seeing that someone in turn. Wolfe and Goodwin are not people, but they are personalities, uniquely entertaining creations, brilliantly written and set. In an ever more homogenized world, both real and fictional, Wolfe and Goodwin are not just different from each other; they remain exceptional from everything else.

Like Charlie Chan, and I never call him "Mr. Chan."

Sources:

Robert Frost, "The Road Not Taken," *Mountain Interval* (1916)

Neal Gabler, *Walt Disney: The Triumph of the American Imagination* (2006)

Alva Johnston, "Alias Nero Wolfe – 1," *New Yorker* (July 16, 1949)

Dr. R. D. Laing, *The Divided Self* (1960)

Alexis Madrigal, *Atlantic*, quoted in "Social-Media Watch: Twitter Is Not America," *New York Post* (April 27, 2019)

John McAleer, *Rex Stout: A Majesty's Life* (2002)

Roberta Schira, "Nero Wolfe: Investigating Appetites," finedininglovers.com (July 2, 2011)

Rex Stout, *The Doorbell Rang* (1965)

> *The Silent Speaker* (1946)

> "Murder Is Corny," *Trio for Blunt Instruments* (1964)

Benjamin Welton, "Eccentricity and Domesticity: The World of the Nero Wolfe Mysteries," *The Imaginative Conservative* (2014)

*Curiously, reading Nero Wolfe and James Beard, side-by-side, each speaking about food, they mirror each other in erudition, style, and viewpoint. I cannot uncover any reported instance of Rex Stout and Beard meeting and discussing food, but the resemblance of their expressed thoughts on this common topic is uncanny and thought-provoking.

II.
The First Film Wolfe

In 1935, Rex Stout sells the film rights for *Fer-de-Lance* (and *The League of Frightened Men*) to Columbia Pictures. The stories are barely one year old, but Hollywood recognizes their appeal and hurries to adapt them for the screen. In a tip to filmgoers, Columbia titles the first film *Meet Nero Wolfe.*

A number of well-known actors are considered for the role of Nero Wolfe, with the producers envisioning a single lead star for both film adaptations. Stout states he prefers Charles Laughton as Wolfe, but Laughton begs off, not wanting to be committed to the role and limit his other film opportunities. Laughton's wife, Elsa Lanchester, observes, "I seem to remember Charles being very interested in the character of Nero Wolfe." Nigel Bruce, who eventually plays the cinematic Dr. Watson to Basil Rathbone's Sherlock Homes, is another potential, along with Alexander Woollcott, who harbors the apparently mistaken belief Stout patterns Wolfe after him, and Walter Connolly, who would play Wolfe in the subsequent film of *The League of Frightened Men*. The combination of Sydney Greenstreet as Wolfe and Humphrey Bogart as Archie is possibly also in consideration. Instead, actor Edward Arnold is cast in the lead for the first film. According to John McAleer, "Columbia's idea was to keep Arnold busy with low-cost Wolfe films between features."

Arnold's initial reaction to being cast is favorable:

"Long before I ever thought I would be cast for Nero Wolfe, I read Rex Stout's story in the *Saturday Evening Post*. At the time, I thought 'What a good picture this would make.'"

Arnold's acting talents cover many memorable performances prior to and after this film. He is an accomplished Broadway actor in the early 1930s, but in 1932 he appears in the film *Okay America* as a gangster and receives a salary "for four days' work" of $900, after a New York stage salary of $400 per week and a "West Coast" salary of $200. He and his wife are convinced motion pictures are a rewarding pursuit for an actor. He goes on to play the doctor in the film *Rasputin and the Empress* (1932), acting with all three Barrymores; a priest in *The White Sister* (1933) with Helen Hayes; a "bibulous" millionaire playboy in *Sadie McKee* (1934) with Joan Crawford; and King Louis XIII with George Arliss in the title role of *Cardinal Richelieu* (1935). Coincidentally, Arnold plays the secretary of war in the 1934 film of Rex Stout's *The President Vanishes*. For Arnold, it is the title role in *Diamond Jim* (1935) that marks his ascension to stardom. He carries the film as the charming and forceful Brady, who is portrayed simultaneously as a business whiz who is also naïve in matters of the heart. Audiences connect with Brady's Horatio Alger rise to financial success and his tragic inability to find the love of his life. Though the film is thin on fact, it is Arnold's sincerity as Brady that makes it a success.

Arnold is a product of a hardworking family and a childhood of limited material circumstances. He says about his growing up, "Kids are not conscious of poverty when everyone around them is living in the same condition." His telling of his life story in his autobiography, *Lorenzo Goes to Hollywood*, demonstrates his life-long lack of artifice, reliance on family values and grounding, and dedication to his craft. The character of Diamond Jim Brady is perfectly fitted to him. He plays the character again in the 1940 film *Lillian Russell*.

The novel *Fer-de-Lance* brings Stout's essential characters to life, and as a consequence, they are still in formation, just beginning their road to maturity. Wolfe speaks a bit too long and at times comes across as pompous and showy. Archie is a bit immature and touchy, somewhat callow though not guileless. Frankly, Archie is finding his voice, but his narration, the story itself, and the attendant characters are fun nonetheless. L. Neil Smith notes, "Archie, who starts as a diamond-in-the-rough tough guy . . . evolves, over the decades, into a sophisticated observer of his own culture." *Fer-de-Lance* is Archie's genesis. Wolfe's dispatching of the killer and the original target is cold-blooded and, alas, reasonable: this is the first time Wolfe manipulates justice in his own hands, and not the last. It isn't random plotting that this, the first Wolfe novel and forty-one years later, *A Family Affair*, the last both end with the killer committing suicide and Wolfe as the avenging angel, if not formally deus ex machina.

The film *Meet Nero Wolfe* is a bittersweet confection for those who appreciate Stout's stories. Lionel Stander acts Archie Goodwin, a court jester paired with his fiancée, Mazie Gray, played by Dennie Moore. The two bounce off each other as co-nitwits; Moore is especially idiotic as a licorice-eating nincompoop with an annoying whine. But Arnold's Wolfe is almost worth tolerating the idiocy. This Wolfe is strong willed, a dominating presence who overcomes a weak Archie and commands the screen in all his scenes. He is stern, docking Archie for a busted lamp that occurs when demonstrating a golf swing and forcing Archie to pay expenses out of his own pocket.

During a sumptuous lunch for the caddies, Wolfe gives Archie a platter of hot dogs. Wolfe laughs at his detractors when the Barstow family and the other suspects visit him and ask that he desist from proclaiming college president Barstow's death a murder. Wolfe even snarls at Olaf, the dour Swedish chef. He spits out the bootleg beer he is sampling because his regular supplier, Maria Maringola (played by attractive, eighteen-year-old Rita Hayworth, billed as "Rita Cansino"), fails to make her customary delivery. O. E. McBride incorrectly states Wolfe drinks hot chocolate in this film as a bow to Prohibition – Wolfe drinks bootleg beer throughout the film and, unfortunately, mostly straight from the bottle, a crassness not in the novel.* He also burps once, ever so gently.

Arnold gives the role his full acting attention, taking a position on how Wolfe should be performed and engaging the performance with a vigor and energy that is outspoken. In light of the desecration of the Archie character and the corners cut by Hollywood, including changing the ending drastically and thereby weakening the story, Arnold's work deserves praise. Except Arnold doesn't see it that way:

"With Nero Wolfe being the character he is, I had the feeling that if he could have been pushed out of the front door of his home once in a while, or forced to take a walk around the block occasionally, the story would have been more valuable as picture material . . . I was surprised that so many audiences seemed to like the play."

Arnold even compares Stout's work with *Crime and Punishment* unfavorably, "only thinking of them both in terms of the screen."

Arnold says he reads *Fer-de-Lance* well before he accepts the role. What, then, is the basis for his disconnect with how the story and characters are written versus his idea for portraying them on film? At the time the film is made, and perhaps to some extent still, Hollywood is ruled by powerful men, titans of the movie industry, men who re-made themselves from tailors and peddlers on the lower end of the socio-economic scale to wealthy taste-makers in California. They are perpetually engaged in re-dressing the truth. They control the stories they peddle, and like garments sold from the backs of trucks, these stories are altered with gewgaws and frilled for general consumption. No property they own is safe from the manipulations of their insular viewpoint of the worlds they boss–such as casting Archie as a clown to provide comic relief in an otherwise serious story because they feel the moviegoing public demands it. Their Hollywood doesn't sell honest ideas. Dismembering the truth is not enough to satisfy their perfidious avarice – everything is bastardized. A working actor of stature accepts this reality and assumes the corporate line. He or she sees the film world as the employer sees it. A cinematic story has its own requisites, no matter the source material, and marketing is paramount. *Meet Nero Wolfe* is given an ending vastly different from Stout's, presumably because 1936 Hollywood can't accept a serving up of murder-suicide and patricide to the public.

Moreover, it may not be reasonable to expect any actor at that time to know how to portray Wolfe in the very first dramatization of the character. Arnold is a moving part in the motion picture business, the talent. He shows up for filming, learns his lines, and hits his marks on the set. Given a part not acted before, he colors the performance within the strict confines of the script, the director's vision, and the studio's intention to make a film that sells. Whatever the prevailing circumstances, Arnold gives what he can to the part but fails to see the final product as satisfactory to his standards. The pity is that likely no other actor at that time would turn in a markedly better performance.

Stout doesn't care for the film, especially Stander's contribution. Sloppy comic relief isn't the author's cup of tea. His hatred of film adaptations of his works dates from this time. Stout tells Michael Bourne, "I detest both TV and moving pictures, and to hell with it."

Many other critics cast their eyes negatively on Arnold's rendition of Wolfe. McBride calls this first Wolfe on film "sternly unlikable." Writer Mark Murphy makes the sage comment that because the screenwriters and director can't replicate Archie's "jaundiced first-person narration," they devise the creative decision "to make Wolfe cranky one moment and jovial the next. Edward Arnold was a good enough actor to get away with this, but the fat guy we're seeing is obviously an impostor." The retrospective article "Nero Wolfe at the Door . . . and Out!" for *Scarlet Street* magazine in 2002 proposes:

"What goes wrong – at least from a purist's standpoint – is the decision to portray Wolfe as a far too jolly character. This is odd in itself, since Arnold was rarely an actor who specialized in projecting good humor."

Other reviewers see merit in Arnold's work and in their way try to counterbalance the negative judgments. *Variety's* review in July 1936 states, "Arnold has contributed lots more than girth and a capacity for beer guzzling. His Nero Wolfe jells suavely with the imagination and makes a piquant example of personality conception." The *New York Times* reviewer in the same month likes the film and makes the suggestion "that Nero Wolfe be permitted in the near future to leave his orchidaceous and beer-soaked flat, if only for a brief visit to the morgue or something," which is just what Wolfe does in the next novel, *The League of Frightened Men*. Dennis Toth, writing the *Film Notes from the Columbus Museum of Art Series* in 2010, avers:

"Edward Arnold as Wolfe, however, was an amply appropriate choice. An excellent character actor, Arnold specialized in playing arrogant, overbearing figures. Plump more than fat,

Arnold made up for his lack of excess poundage by zeroing in on Wolfe's domineering personality."

How the viewer sees the character of Nero Wolfe is dictated by how the viewer appraises Arnold's capacity to play Wolfe believably. Believability hinges on the viewer's knowledge of the original character. The viewer less acquainted with the written character is more open to Arnold's film interpretation. Perhaps it is prudent to say Nero Wolfe is too new in 1936 to develop a fixed cinematic persona or a totally rounded literary one. The unfortunate rejection by Arnold to reprise the role in *The League of Frightened Men* means viewers will never know how he might or would grow into the character.

In 1942 Arnold plays the blind detective Duncan Maclain in *Eyes in the Night* for MGM. His assistant is Marty, acted by Allen Jenkins, whose character is somewhat toned down from Lionel Stander's Archie Goodwin, but by increments. In this film, Jenkins shares the comic relief duties with Mantan Moreland as Alistair, the butler. Moreland, a frequent sidekick to Charlie Chan, is expert at producing laughs on the screen. He is a comedian. His ethnic stereotyping, however, is immodest as seen in modern terms, but it is lucrative employment for him at the time. Arnold's performance is crisp and convincing, and he follows it in 1945 with playing Maclain again in *The Hidden Eye*, also for MGM. The very last line in the 1942 film is probably a reference to Arnold's starring role in *Meet Nero Wolfe* six years previously. When Alistair catches Friday, the wonder dog assistant to Maclain, fooling around with a female dog, he exclaims, "You wolf!"

Sources:

Edward Arnold, *Lorenzo Goes to Hollywood* (1940)

Michael Bourne interview with Rex Stout (July 18, 1973)

Dick Lochte, "Beyond the Book: Nero Wolfe," mysteryscenemagazine.com

John T. MacManus, "'Meet Nero Wolfe' Brings a New and Engaging Gumshoe to the Rivoli, " *New York Times* (July 26, 1936)

John McAleer, *Rex Stout: A Majesty's Life* (2002)

O. E. McBride, *Stout Fellow: A Guide Through Nero Wolfe's World* (2003)

Mark Murphy, "At the (Old) Movies: 'Meet Nero Wolfe,'" *Murphy's Craw* (October 24, 2012)

L. Neil Smith, "'Intelligence Guided by Experience' A Brief Look at Rex Stout's Nero Wolfe," *Libertarian Enterprise*, no. 68 (March 31, 2002)

Rex Stout, *Fer-de-Lance* (1934)

Dennis Toth, "The Great Detectives," *Film Notes from the Columbus Museum of Arts Series* (April 10, 2010)

Richard Valley (editor), "Nero Wolfe at the Door . . . and Out!," *Scarlet Street*, no. 46 (2002)

"Meet Nero Wolfe," *Variety* (July 22, 1936)

Eyes in the Night, MGM (1942)

Meet Nero Wolfe, Columbia Pictures (1936)

*McBride is confusing *Meet Nero Wolfe* with the 1937 film *The League of Frightened Men*, where Walter Connolly as Wolfe does indeed sip hot chocolate exclusively and unconvincingly on screen.

III.
Late Review:
The League of Frightened Men –
the Book, the Film, the Dark Matter

Rex Stout writes *The League of Frightened Men* in late 1934, immediately after the publication of his first Nero Wolfe novel, *Fer-de-Lance*. Published in 1935, *The League of Frightened Men* picks up the lives and adventures of Wolfe, Goodwin, and the rest where the introductory novel leaves off, and in fine style.

Looking retrospectively over the body of Wolfe stories, *The League of Frightened Men* is one of Stout's darkest. The backdrop is a decades-old college hazing that takes a cruel turn, leaving a poor student permanently crippled. To add to the story's dark quality, the hazers, ashamed of their actions, contribute to their victim's support in a gallant and pathetic "atonement." They become the League of Atonement. As they mature, the atoners believe they are forgiven. One of their number dies in a mysterious fall, and soon another dies, allegedly as a suicide. The victim of the college hazing, writer Paul Chapin, responds to the League's past charity by now mailing each of his former classmates poems hailing the deaths in their number, deaths of which Chapin may or may not be the perpetrator. It is a perverse, tangled, and deeply disturbing psychological dance of the macabre. This perversity is exacerbated by one of the former classmates, Professor Hibbard, disappearing, seemingly into thin air, prompting the surviving fellows to eventually enlist Wolfe to protect them from Chapin, a man reduced to limping on a cane to walk. In this case, Wolfe actually solicits his clients (after reading Chapin's books to understand him), convincing them to sign an agreement to pay him should he remove the threat of Chapin based on a vote of the group. They now become the League of Frightened Men. The notions that Chapin may not be the real menace, that his former classmates cringe in terror at the thought of him creeping along to kill them, one by one, and the obvious delight Chapin finds in all this, mark *The League of Frightened Men* as darker fictional material than Stout attempts in most other Wolfe stories. (*Fer-de-Lance* does prominently feature severe domestic violence and a murderous hatred between father and son.) The specter of the Depression pervades the book, as does the strange, perhaps sexless marriage of Chapin and his wife Dora, (the former maid of the woman for whom Chapin has a fetishistic longing as the wife of one of the atoners, the woman whom Wolfe calls "Chapin's unattainable"). On first sight, Archie reports of Dora, "They don't come any uglier." Wolfe and Archie meet Dora Chapin when she visits the brownstone unannounced and reveals she has been cut by her husband, in an attempt, in Archie's words "to cut her head off." Dora explains Chapin did it to her because "he wanted to kill me" during one of his "cold fits." Wolfe quickly determines the wounds are self-inflicted and amateurishly so. Dark business all around.

Prior to 1934, Rex Stout writes several works that dig into psychologically dark matter. *Under the Andes* in 1914 finds three barely clothed humans, two men and a woman, trapped in subterranean earth, battling grotesquely deformed Incas in near darkness to survive and escape. The story suggests sexual episodes involving the female and the ruler of the sub-humans, as well as a romantic triangle among the humans. It is tediously written, but the ending has a curious and disturbing twist. According to its cover, *How Like a God* in 1929 concerns "a sexual psychotic – his strange marriage, abnormal obsessions and dark desires." Stout describes it as three hundred pages of a man "talking to himself," mostly about sex, while climbing the stairs to kill someone, perhaps his wife or himself. It is Stout's first serious novel and the first published in book form. *Seed on the Wind* in 1930 is a "sex novel," where the seed is sperm cast in many directions.

The League of Frightened Men takes many of these accumulated dark elements and weaves them seamlessly into a successful Wolfe story – jealousy, obsession, incapacitation, pity, sex, and lack of same, unfulfilled desire, guilty conscience, vengeance, morbid fear, perverted fantasy, murder. David Anderson labels the book as built around "a case of fetishism." The *New York Times* dubs it "everything a good detective story should have – mystery, suspense, action . . . a pleasure to read."

The story takes the reader through the search for the missing Professor Hibbard, the discovery of Chapin's fetish box, Archie being drugged, and Wolfe leaving the brownstone. With all these facets, what stimulates the reader's appetite and attention is Archie's clear and distinctive voice as narrator. This is the second Wolfe book: the precedents of character, setting, pacing, and personality are in place, and now Stout must both replicate them and build for the future. The series becomes a long-term success because of the delivery of *Fer-de-Lance*, followed by this book, establishing Nero Wolfe through Archie's eyes, attracting and then maintaining enthralled readers. Both books are still, more than eighty years later, much respected and read by fans and critics.

The book's climax is smart. Wolfe produces an alive Professor Hibbard to the relief of his friends. (When Wolfe unmasks him earlier in the story, hiding in the disguise of a vagabond, Hibbard delivers a razor-sharp critique of the academic discipline of psychology, no doubt from Stout's own beliefs.) Wolfe removes any suspicion of Chapin by displaying a forged non-confession and, in need of funds, asks the League to pay the bill per their agreement with him. When they balk, and only because they balk, Wolfe pulls back the curtain on the real killer sitting among them, a killer without the exciting dark motive of vengeance, but one of simple, tawdry greed. In punishment for possessing one of Chapin's fetishes and for forging the non-confession, Chapin promises to kill Wolfe as a character in his next book "in the most abhorrent manner conceivable." The League is no longer frightened.

Stout's overwhelming disdain for filming his works is only on the horizon in 1935, at which time he agrees to sell the rights to both of his first two Wolfe novels to Hollywood for a cool $15,000 total, significant cash in 1935 dollars, approximately $276,000 in 2019. Stout participates in discussions about who should play the lead role; he favors casting Charles Laughton, but the actor can't dedicate himself to a series. Walter Connolly gets the Wolfe role in *The League of Frightened Men* in 1936 because *Meet Nero Wolfe*'s (*Fer-de-Lance* on film in 1935) star Edward Arnold won't commit to the second film. Stout's subsequent disdain of the visual media dates from the appearance of these first two films.

That disdain is fully understandable. The film *The League of Frightened Men* can be dissected into three parts:

- Lionel Stander's Archie, acting like a fool.
- The unforgivably wretched performance by Walter Connolly.
- The essential plot elements from the book.

The easiest one to deal with is the first. Stander's performance in the first Wolfe film is beyond bad, but he has a sidekick, his fiancée, as a foil, and that somehow makes his part less offensive, as she also shoulders the blame. One fool needs another fool so as not to be alone. Edward Arnold as the lead in *Meet Nero Wolfe* is a strong enough actor to dominate any shared scenes with the two dimwits, easing some of the misery of watching their performances. In the second film, every needless, exhausting, distracting, brainless moment belongs solely to Stander, and he performs down to that level in every minute of screen time. Archie is not of Middle European descent, raised in an urban ethnic enclave; Stander is, and he plays Archie in that mode. Stander's guttural rumblings as Archie are fingernails scratched over a blackboard, out of place and jarring. Do audiences in the theaters at that time really enjoy this? One would have to find an audience member from then still alive to determine. Not likely. To avoid applying current standards of popular taste to a bygone era, it is best to say cutting every one of Stander's scenes or cutting him out of all the other scenes would neither shorten the film considerably nor harm the film's quality or continuity noticeably. In fact, it might be an improvement. This is not fault to be laid at Stander's feet. At the time he is one of the highest paid character actors in Hollywood. His portrayal is a decision by the screenwriter, producer, and director, and they all get it wrong. In this role, he is the quintessential knucklehead tough guy. No brains, all bluster.

Walter Connolly as Nero Wolfe is Columbia Pictures' second choice for the lead. The producers want Edward Arnold to return, but he isn't interested. Connolly should be third choice, because anyone else would be noticeably better. In a role that demands gravitas and weight, a large-sized man with a large-sized ego and personality, Connolly is a pip-squeak. He squeaks with a faux upper-class cast of voice, much like a maître d' on a third-rate cruise ship. In this part he is akin to an unfunny comedian acting English high drama in a traveling carnival show. He's an imitation of an imitation. Connolly's Wolfe is so light in his loafers that he floats through the scenes. He is not believable as anything but a dandy in aspic. In addition, he is rather handsy, with his fey demeanor, touching people left and right. This characterization is Connolly's responsibility to bear and the audience's to suffer. While Wolfe in his dressing gown sips hot chocolate (drinking beer straight from the bottle, as in the first film, is banished), Archie is comfortable, feet up in an easy chair, reading the newspaper and begging like a teenager about wanting to go to the movies. He refuses Wolfe's offer of chocolate twice because "it makes me burp." Wolfe simpers that he wants to stay in with his chocolate, books, and music (no mention of orchids, though they do make a brief appearance late in the film). Apparently, the two of them are date buddies. This Wolfe shakes hands, fiddles with the sash of his silk dressing gown, offers his guest a cigar, and himself smokes cigarettes. At film's end, Wolfe rushes out the door "to get myself a drink."

The other member of Wolfe's brownstone household is Butch, the butler. By Archie, Butch is a "slug-nutty pug," recently out of the slammer and hired by Wolfe as a sort of rehabilitation project by the self-proclaimed "America's best private investigator . . . no false modesty about me, you see." Gone after *Meet Nero Wolfe* is Olaf, the Swedish chef and film stand-in for Fritz Brenner. (The "List of Players" for *The League of Frightened Men* shows a character "Fritz" played by Herbert Ashley, but he is not in Wolfe's household.) Surrounding Connolly's cheaply sophisticated Wolfe with two ruffians is done to make the Wolfe character appear more eccentric, civilized, and cultured. This probably reflects the producer's prejudiced view of the world or mistaken view of what makes audiences appreciate what Wolfe represents. Wolfe is neither a gadfly nor an arriviste: he is a genius and an artist.

Eduardo Ciannelli, an Italian-born character actor and baritone, plays Paul Chapin as fittingly creepy and seething with barely concealed rage at what life deals him. He propels himself on two canes, although the book only prescribes one, and in doing so, moving ever haltingly and straight ahead. His screen presence is at once menacing, bold, and full of pathos. You see how grim and molten-hot angry he is; even with literary acclaim he remains physically limited but defiant. The performance stands out in such an otherwise mediocre film.* In Wolfe's office, surrounded by his classmates, Chapin, leaning on his canes, sardonically intones, "Life is much too short to be wasted," with a sneer. On his jail cell cot, Chapin in a cold fury, dismisses Inspector Cramer's badgering. He is enjoying his notoriety as the suspected killer, a deed he could not accomplish outside of his books. This is a savvy translation on film of one of Stout's darkest characters.

The members of the League are capably acted. Leonard Mudie looks terrified as Hibbard, and Walter Kingsford's Bowen is a well-dressed lizard.**

A more substantial lead actor and the subtraction of Stander's Archie would yield a better film. In spite of which, the film follows almost all of Stout's original plot elements and does so admirably. Whoever is the script doctor for this second Hollywood try at Wolfe decides to lighten the lead role, amp up the comic relief, and exit Olaf, but stick to Stout's core story. Getting the basics right, that person undoes the film's potential success by burdening it with disfiguring nonessentials and muggery. The film version of *The League of Frightened Men* is a curio, worth viewing for its oddities and what it says to viewers about its time and place. Like a spectacular car wreck, you shouldn't stare, but you can't help yourself and your curiosity. Maybe just one look. Is it worth it? Perhaps.

Sources:

David R. Anderson, *Rex Stout* (1984)

Michael Bourne interview with Rex Stout (July 18, 1973)

John McAleer, *Rex Stout: A Majesty's Life* (2002)

James L. Neibaur, *The Charlie Chan Films* (2018)

Rex Stout, *Under the Andes* (1914)

    How Like a God (1929)

    Seed on the Wind (1930)

    Fer-de-Lance (1934)

    The League of Frightened Men (1935)

Meet Nero Wolfe, Columbia Pictures (1936)

The League of Frightened Men, Columbia Pictures (1937)

*Ciannelli acted professionally for fifty-two years; one notable example of his late work can be seen in the *Burke's Law* episode "Who Killed the Tall One in the Middle," first aired November 25, 1964, in which the intensity of his performance far outdistances his brief time on screen.

**Mudie would play a murder victim in 1940's *Charlie Chan's Murder Cruise* and a thespian named Horace Karlos in the 1945 Charlie Chan film *The Scarlet Clue*. Perhaps his most notable screen roles were the title character in the 1934 film *The Mystery of Mr. X* and De Bourenne in *Anthony Adverse* (1936). Walter Kingsford's prominent screen role was Dr. P. Walter Carew in the Dr. Kildare film series (1938-1945).

IV.
An Archie Goodwin Quintet

Archie Goodwin, the essential character in the Wolfe stories, is acted in the American film and television media by five men from 1936 to 2002:

- Lionel Stander – *Meet Nero Wolfe* (1936) and *The League of Frightened Men* (1937)

- William Shatner – *Nero Wolfe,* "Count the Man Down" (1959)

- Tom Mason – *Nero Wolfe* (1977)

- Lee Horsley – *Rex Stout's Nero Wolfe* (1981)

- Timothy Hutton – *A Nero Wolfe Mystery* (2000–2002)

Each actor makes an imprint on the role, the first three in brief appearances. Horsley and Hutton have the opportunity to give more lasting performances – Horsley for fourteen episodes acting with television veteran William Conrad as Nero Wolfe, and Hutton for one pilot film and twenty episodes with Maury Chaykin as Wolfe. Hutton is also an executive producer and for four episodes (two of which are double episodes) the director. Stander acts in two Wolfe feature films, pairing with Edward

Arnold in 1936 and Walter Connolly in 1937. Shatner works with Kurt Kasznar as Nero Wolfe, and Mason pairs with Thayer David in pilot episodes.

(On December 9, 1956, Rex Stout, despite his hostility toward the "goddamn" visual medium, appears on television's *Omnibus* program in "The Fine Art of Murder," with actors Gene Reynolds and Robert Eckles acting respectively as Goodwin and Wolfe. The appearance is short and entails Stout commenting on, and the actors performing, a set sketch about how Nero Wolfe would solve a mystery. This brief dramatization is not included in the instant discussion.)

These five actors are about as disparate a collection of talents as could be assembled. Only Shatner and Hutton achieve star status. The remaining three are supporting players, and of them, Stander is the lone established character actor. Hutton occupies the star rung above that, previously winning an Oscar for Best Performance by a Supporting Actor. Shatner is a star, with Broadway credits, building a respected career long after his 1959 turn as Archie. Mason and Horsley are basically television actors, though both have big screen credits as well.

Rather than reviewing and critiquing the company of actors who translate Nero Wolfe on screen (large and small), it is this gallery of a quintet of Archie Goodwin actors that merits attention first. Goodwin is described mostly by himself in the stories as younger than Wolfe, far more physically active, and an admirer of the companionship of women – in short, Wolfe's opposite. Rex Stout describes Archie as:

> "Height six feet. Weight 180 pounds ... Hair is light rather than dark, but just barely decided not to be red: he gets it cut every two weeks, rather short, and brushes it straight back, but it keeps standing up . . . His features are all regular, well-modeled and proportioned, except

the nose . . . it is a little short and the ridge is broad, and the tip has continued on its own . . . The eyes are grey (and hard), and are inquisitive and quick to move. He is muscular . . . and upright in posture . . ."

In his essay "Gentleman Don Juan," Wolfe enthusiast Rev. Frederick G. Gotwald says of Archie, "men envy him and women adore [him]." In a reflection on the Wolfe-Goodwin combination, Gotwald deduces the relationship "grows over [the] period of their collaboration in the detective business. It moves from employer-employee, Father/Son, to Man-to-Man." We have a fair picture that between Wolfe and Goodwin at last is a sense of equality and mutual respect. Neither person can accomplish his mission without the other.

In Stout's obituary in the *New York Times*, Alden Whitman describes Archie Goodwin as "a brash but efficient legman." The legendary critic Jacques Barzun calls Archie Goodwin one of the most memorable characters in American literature.

It is worth a ponder, then, how this quintet of Archie performers measures up to the Goodwin standard.

Lionel Stander is a veteran actor appearing in dozens of American and European films, and does extensive television work later in his career, from 1928 to 1994. The term "handsome" clearly does not fit him – his mouth and lips are not proportionate to his face, and his Bronx accent from birth is with him to the end. By no stretch is he a physical proxy for the Archie standard. Stander is fit but, head to toe, not well proportioned. Stander's screen forte is the street-smart tough guy, wisecracking through fights and tight spots. But men envy him and women adore him? Not likely. He is a second banana for sure, but not in the Archie mold of mutual respect with number one.

Speculating over eighty years afterward, his selection as Archie Goodwin in 1936 and 1937 seems linked to his acting history of sidekick roles and perhaps a producer's vision to add humor to the Wolfe films. Stander adds nothing of creative value or substance to *Meet Nero Wolfe* or *The League of Frightened Men* except buffoonery. His gravely nasal Bronx accent and mispronunciations are major distractions from the storyline, cheapening the film's dramatic quality; however, a perusal of similar detective fiction films of the era uncovers the same production wisdom of injecting comic relief and even musical numbers to lighten the mood. Many of the Charlie Chan films, for example, contain broad swatches of comedy and forays into popular songs by pretty singers as part of the plots. This now seems wrong on many levels, but back then, it probably sells tickets. In *Variety* on July 22, 1936, an unnamed reviewer calls this Archie portrayal "a typical mugg role for Stander" and Stander's contribution an "important entertainment factor in the film." That is *Variety*-speak for comic relief. Film historian Jon Tuska declares, "Unhappily, Lionel Stander's Archie in *The League of Frightened Men* is far too much of a bungler." And a fool.

Rex Stout is displeased with the actor's performances as Archie in both films. Instead of a man-to-man relationship between Wolfe and Archie, or even a father-to-son, Stander to both actors playing Wolfe is court jester-to-king. To be fair, Stander the person is evidently glib, strong willed, and a believer in his own high ideals. He addresses government questions about his political ideologies before the House Un-American Activities Committee with candor and wit, admitting he does stand for left-wing causes without groveling. He is simply the wrong actor for Archie Goodwin, further burdened by a pitiful script (at the film's end, Archie and his girlfriend get married and set their honeymoon for Coney Island!).

The young William Shatner is devilishly close to an Archie-type. His eyes are indeed quick and inquisitive, his mouth nicely formed, although his hair is dark and slick. Yes, men do envy him, and women are attracted. (Now in his late age, Shatner still has those qualities.) His voice is sharp and distinctive, clipped, and pleasant. He is physically fit and upright. Shatner is twenty-eight years old during the filming, and both he and Kasznar are stars of the Broadway stage. Though it is difficult, and maybe unfair, to judge by one pilot film, Shatner and Kasznar's Wolfe look comfortable with each other – not completely man-to-man, less father-to-son, but not entirely employer-to-employee. Shatner's performance makes a lot out of a thin script, as does Kasznar's, motivating the viewer to wish there is more to come. In fact, *Baltimore Sun* television critic Donald Kirkley at the time points out that the pilot is "considered too good to be confined to half an hour." That is a direct result of the quality of the acting. Shatner's Archie, in particular, is nobody's fool.

Tom Mason's portrayal is marred by his youthful appearance, relative inexperience, and a crummy script. He can't escape the utter disaster of Frank Gilroy's *Nero Wolfe*. Mason doesn't project maturity in a role that requires a solid mature presence. Mason and David do come across as father-to-son, but not in a dignified way: Mason's Goodwin spends the film totally out of his depth, except for a few minor scenes. David's sotto voce, throwaway asides praising Goodwin seem gratuitous. Acting next to David's scene-eating as Wolfe does Mason's efforts no favors. Not having Archie as the narrator does the viewer no favor. It is a mismatch – an overbearing lead drowning a supporting actor in the shallow end of the pool. The imbalance could be alleviated somewhat if Archie is telling the story, observing and commenting as it unfolds. Physically, Mason looks lost in his clothes. No grown man envies him, and only female college sophomores and motherly types want him. He couldn't buy a date. (Sorry, Tom.) Mason's Archie isn't a fool, but he is a *nayfish*, a doormat.

Stare into Lee Horsley's eyes and you find a man who knows he can definitely be adored. He is a stereotypical man's man, filling out his clothes with masculine charm and a polished toughness. He passes the envy-adore test with high marks. The Wolfe-Goodwin relationship between Horsley and Conrad is some point in the middle of employer-to-employee and man-to-man, skipping the father-to-son part. There is no father-to-son with them. That might be the big flaw in this dynamic: Horsley's Archie seems headstrong in one direction, Conrad's Wolfe in another. It is as if Archie is running his own detective business alongside Wolfe's. They lack noticeable professional affection for each other and a shared passion. Wolfe wants to play inside, and Archie needs to get out into the street. The series' writing and direction sees Wolfe as the hidebound, housebound eccentric and Archie as the rough-and-tumble outside operative, but not as a team. Horsley could have his own spin-off, *Lee Horsley as Archie Goodwin*, and the stories would be the same.

Obviously, that doesn't work in this context. There is no Wolfe without Goodwin and no Goodwin without Wolfe. Horsley's performance is acceptable but not satisfying. According to Horsley, "I think we [Conrad and he] played it a little more tongue in cheek [than the books] but that is really what made it so much fun." In sum, Horsley is a proficient television actor and so is Conrad, but together they don't work in the tenor of the Wolfe stories. This flaw is magnified again by the absence of Archie's narration. Horsley's Archie is tough enough and resourceful, but he's not a fit with even Conrad's version of Wolfe.

Timothy Hutton knows Archie Goodwin. He proudly states he has read "just about all" the stories. Having done his homework, he feels "pretty comfortable about what the Nero world needed to look like and how the dialogue should be played." His performance as Archie reflects the care he takes with the role and the series' loving attention to the unique Wolfe-Goodwin relationship and the body of Stout's work. Hutton comments:

> "They get on each other's nerves quite a bit. They come from different worlds and yet there's a huge mutual respect and admiration and trust, particularly from Nero to Archie."

Hutton quotes Wolfe from *Champagne for One,* "Our tolerance of each other is a recurring miracle." Goodwin states in *The League of Frightened Men,* "Sometimes I thought it was a wonder that Wolfe and I got on together at all."

This care and attention are all the more fruitful in the production because, unlike his predecessors, Hutton's Archie is the narrator. If you trust Hutton's performance, you trust Archie Goodwin. There are criticisms that Hutton's Archie has a New York accent, whereas Goodwin is a son of Ohio. Pfui. People who live long enough immersed in the big city often develop the city's oral cadences and pronunciations, as well as its manners. Especially Archie, who spends his time mingling with New York's upper, middle, and lower crusts. It's his living. Hutton describes the stories' dialogue as "Damon Runyon meets Noel Coward."

Envy-adore? Hutton has it. Physicality? He meets the standard. He even has a touch of bad-boy in his eyes. One viewer enthuses, "Timothy Hutton *is* Archie Goodwin." He embodies Archie so thoroughly, "it has now become impossible to read the books without hearing Hutton's voice as the narrator." Hutton's swagger in Archie's walk fits in character.

Hutton is ably surrounded by a potent cast, with emphasis on the late Maury Chaykin as Wolfe. Excepting Chaykin's occasional shouting, which should be theatrical bellowing to truly effect the stories' tone, he displays the facial expressions, tics, and bits of eccentricity that define Wolfe. Hutton and Chaykin sustain their performances from start to finish. Hutton's Archie is the one Wolfe wants by his side.

Together they are the embodiment of Rex Stout's invention. What would Stout think of them? That is impossible to guess. One hopes the storyteller would recognize the quality and fidelity of their performances, striving to match his own excellence. Like a mother's attitude about a treasured child, Stout might not find any re-creation up to his appreciation. One wishes the Quaker-born Stout somewhere now looks upon what is crafted under his name and finds a smile or two. Maybe he's talking with the bluff Stander about it all over cigars and glasses of brandy. Does Stander smoke? Are there cigars and brandy in the next life? Stay tuned.

Sources:

Michael Bourne interview with Rex Stout (July 18, 1973)

"The Fine Art of Murder," www.Fampeople.com

Rev. Frederick G. Gotwald, *The Nero Wolfe Handbook* (1995)

Mitchel Hedley, "Mitchel's Top Ten, #7: Nero Wolfe," www. itsabouttv (August 27, 2013)

Donald Kirkley, "Look and Listen with Donald Kirkley," *Baltimore Sun* (January 26, 1959)

Steven Linan, "For Hutton It's All About Language and Style," *Los Angeles Times* (April 20, 2001)

John McAleer, *Rex Stout: A Majesty's Life* (2002)

"Meet Nero Wolfe," *Variety* (July 22, 1936)

Brian Sheridan, www.thefedoralounge (July 10, 2008)

Rex Stout, *The League of Frightened Men* (1935)

Terry Teachout, "A Nero as Hero," *National Review* (August 12, 2001)

Jon Tuska, *The Detective in Hollywood* (1978)

Alden Whitman, "Rex Stout, Creator of Nero Wolfe, Dead," *New York Times* (October 28, 1975)

Meet Nero Wolfe, Columbia Pictures (1936)

The League of Frightened Men, Columbia Pictures (1937)

Nero Wolfe, "Count the Man Down," CBS (1959)

Nero Wolfe, Paramount Television (1977)

Rex Stout's Nero Wolfe, Paramount Television (1981)

A Nero Wolfe Mystery, A & E (2000-2002)

V.
The Subject Was Wolfe:
The Novel, a Book, and Two Films

The Doorbell Rang is one of Rex Stout's most memorable and celebrated stories. Nero Wolfe's gargantuan intellect and ego are pitted against J. Edgar Hoover's monolithic bureaucracy in a match of strategies and wills. When Mrs. Bruner first proposes Wolfe take the assignment, "Now he's annoying me and I want him stopped. I want you to stop him," Wolfe's one-word response is, "Preposterous." He is well aware that few people stop Hoover's FBI, and even Wolfe's giant-sized self-regard can't blind him to the meager possibilities. After escorting Mrs. Bruner to her Rolls-Royce, Archie returns to the office and conveys his opinion of the proposed case with "she'll just have to endure her afflictions, *as you said.*"

Mrs. Bruner, who comments to Wolfe early on, "I know a great deal about you," does indeed know the ways to motivate Wolfe: his self-esteem and his overwhelming need to satisfy his pleasures. She opens the door to clinching him by saying, "I thought you were afraid of nobody and nothing."

Though Wolfe parries with one of his quotable retorts, "Afraid? I can dodge folly without backing into fear," the reader now knows Wolfe is going to take the bait and apply himself (and Archie) to her problem. She seals the deal by replacing her $50,000 check with one for $100,000 – a sum that in 1965, the year of publication, is almost fifteen times greater than the median family income of all Americans. With his pride, appetite, wallet, and wit so tempted, how can Wolfe refuse?

It is indicative of Stout's writing prowess that he begins *The Doorbell Rang* with a foreshadowing of what and why his renowned detective is embarking on this quest:

"Since it was the deciding factor, I might as well begin by describing it. It was a pink slip of paper three inches wide and seven inches long . . ."

The closer, yes, but not the clincher. Mrs. Bruner's massage of Wolfe's ego is the clincher. As a real estate tycoon, or at least the widow of one, she knows the art of the deal.

In 1966, speaking before a gathering of authors, Rex Stout talks about why he wrote *The Doorbell Rang*. The book's public notice starts well in advance of publication when various media outlets learn it is going to be about Wolfe versus the FBI, and they seek interviews with the author. In his biography *Rex Stout: A Majesty's Life,* John McAleer reports that Stout, speaking at a regional conference for women writers in 1964, gives the audience a parting tease about the coming book: "It's created a helluva stink about the FBI and J. Edgar Hoover." Stout's publisher orders an initial printing of double the number of books than indicated by previous bookstore sales. The book is primed to be a best seller. Yet in his 1966 speech, Stout disclaims the idea that taking on the FBI is his primary motivation for the book: "I decided to use a new one [Wolfe antagonist]. I just thought it would be fun [rather than opposing Cramer, the

NYPD, the Westchester County District Attorney, etc.].'' A simple and straightforward writer's motivation. Stout, however, does comment that he read Fred Cook's book, *The FBI Nobody Knows*, and is interested in it. Stout is quoted as calling Hoover "a megalomaniac." Perhaps Stout makes full disclosure when he states in October 1965, "I didn't think of *The Doorbell Rang* as an attack on the FBI while I was writing it." An attack, maybe not, but a head-on criticism, certainly. "A poke in the nose," Stout calls it. There is little doubt Stout writes Wolfe as Stout when Wolfe states his agreement with Cook's opinion of the FBI, "With some minor qualifications, yes," and his mostly negative opinion of J. Edgar Hoover, "Yes." Stout's political opinions are what at that time are categorized as liberal, analogous to, say, John F. Kennedy, Harry Truman, and Eleanor Roosevelt. In sum, Hoover, and by extension his FBI, are dangerously powerful and unchecked, intruding upon and often trampling the civil liberties of the citizens the FBI is sworn to defend and protect.

It is evident in *The FBI Nobody Knows* that Cook is thoroughly versed in his subject. He makes no claims that aren't documented fully, though the reader may at points disagree with his interpretations and conclusions. He is an investigative journalist with a conservative to centrist reputation, who is unafraid to go where his research leads him, without regard for political bent. During his career he is involved in a controversy of his own, being once questioned by the New York District Attorney's Office for a suspicious allegation of being offered a bribe by certain New York City officials. *The FBI Nobody Knows* opens with an FBI agent relating his tenure at the bureau, and his progressive disappointment and disillusion with what he experiences. Cook continues with a history of the bureau and of Hoover. He delves into the Alger Hiss case, which he says found Hiss mistakenly guilty of espionage against the United States; the government's efforts to hunt spies during the World

War eras; and the Cold War period. He ends his book with his indictment of the bureau's behavior:

> "The greatest sin of Hoover and the FBI is that, by a monumental propaganda effort, they have made themselves sacrosanct."

Reading *The FBI Nobody Knows,* it is no wonder Rex Stout is intrigued by it. It must be tempting to Stout, and his surrogates Wolfe and Goodwin, to read, "No man wishes to court the scowl of the FBI" – exactly what Wolfe and Goodwin do all the time with the police departments and district attorneys of New York City and Westchester County. The book is a red flag waved under a creative nose. Challenge accepted.

Hoover's reputation remains generally tarnished on this basis (and others), and it is still haunted by false rumors (significant among them the fantastical belief that he is homosexual, based on the veneer of a drunken socialite's lies) and harsh truths (he ignores organized crime in the 1950s and 1960s and he hounds civil rights defenders ruthlessly, much to the nation's detriment). To this day, the name "J. Edgar Hoover" unfairly represents pure evil to many. Self-serving, sometimes vicious, generally bigoted, and increasingly narrow minded he is, but also patriotic, dedicated, and vigilant, especially during his early tenure as FBI director. His later years are more fairly characterized negatively than those at the beginning of his career when he built the FBI into a modern professional crime-fighting organization. Stout himself remarks, "That man Hoover was really a remarkable man, in some ways a very contemptible and condemnable man, and in some ways he was damned efficient and damned competent."

Not everyone agrees with Cook and Stout's assessment of Hoover's FBI. In a short and sharply written note to Stout by John Wayne after reading *The Doorbell Rang,* the actor says, "Goodbye." Notwithstanding, Hoover and the arrogant

FBI of the 1960s are prime targets for Stout's rapier pen and Wolfe's abilities to deliver the deserved comeuppance. *The Doorbell Rang* is deftly wrought. The plot's singular elegance is that the murder within the story is not the story's objective. It is an accessory to the more exciting story, finding the logic and defending the truth. It is one of the best examples of the qualitative difference between the body of Wolfe stories and any other collection of detective fiction. Wolfe finds the truth; others find killers or thieves. The story is told that when clarinetist Artie Shaw is asked about what separates him from erstwhile rival clarinetist Benny Goodman, Shaw remarks, "Benny Goodman plays the clarinet; I play music." So to Wolfe.

Two-thirds into the book the reader knows who the killer of Morris Althaus is. If it is a surprise at all, it is a mild one. The methods Archie uses to expose the killer are clever and involve him committing a handful of crimes himself – breaking and entering, tampering with potential evidence, lying to the police, and so on. A day's work for Archie. The triumph of having the killer arrested is muted by the clues along the path of the story that Archie might have a physical attraction to this person (described by him early in the story as "a face that rated a glance" and a double entendre comment about frisking her) he successfully brings to justice. But what the reader is waiting for is Wolfe to earn his fee in this preposterous undertaking. He has to untangle the interests of Inspector Cramer and FBI Special Agent in Charge Wragg and then realign them to tie up the case with a pretty bow. Lest we forget, this is all in the service of getting the FBI out of Mrs. Bruner's life! To call this story a neat package is to call champagne a lovely little beverage.

If you haven't yet read the book, do. Knowing some of the finale doesn't spoil it. If you have read it, read it again. It is worth the reacquaintance. It is a master's work, and it hasn't aged a day. The best writing is like that – evergreen.

Twice the wizards of American television try to dramatize *The Doorbell Rang* for broadcast. First at it is Frank Gilroy for Paramount Television, with a made-for-television film titled *Nero Wolfe* in 1977. Gilroy writes and directs. It features Thayer David as Wolfe, Tom Mason as Goodwin, Anne Baxter as Mrs. Bruner, and Brooke Adams as Sarah Dacos. The two-hour film is made on a then generous budget of $1.5 million.

Gilroy is an accomplished playwright and director: among his works are the multi-award-winning play *The Subject Was Roses* and the television series *Burke's Law* (1963-1966). It appears the combination of Paramount and, according to Gilroy's own admission, working with Orson Welles (for whom Paramount bought rights to produce *Nero Wolfe*) attract him to the Nero Wolfe project. The hefty budget is doubtless another lure. Though Welles bowed out of the project (variously attributed to his dislike of television work, his disagreement about the Wolfe characterization, or his inability to learn his lines), Gilroy remains and casts Thayer David for the lead. Gilroy reports that post-Welles, he becomes "acquainted . . . with just about every corpulent middle-aged actor available" before picking David. Then he sits at the typewriter and tosses off the screenplay that he will also direct.

Only Gilroy, long gone to his reward, can explain why he decides to drastically rewrite Stout's story. Haste? Vanity? Gilroy owns the ultimate awards in theater – a playwriting Pulitzer Prize, a Broadway Tony, and an Off-Broadway Obie – and a Berlin International Film Festival award. All Stout has is the undying loyalty and appreciation of his readers. From a removed perspective, one might speculate that Gilroy's recognitions are for relatively transitory works, while Stout's are earned by generations of sustained quality. Not to judge one above the other, but the dissimilarity is evident.

In his diary/memoir *I Wake Up Screening*, Gilroy devotes a scant ten lines and a footnote to his work in *The Doorbell Rang*. He remembers the late Thayer David as "the most widely educated and best-read actor" he knows. He says David's portrayal of Wolfe is "acknowledged the best" by the Nero Wolfe literary society at the time.

At the 2001 Black Orchid Banquet of the Nero Wolfe literary society, Michael Jaffe, executive producer of *A Nero Wolfe Mystery* on A & E, tells his piece of the story about Orson Welles and the television Nero Wolfe. Jaffe doesn't state specifically if these events happen prior to the 1977 film or if the producer he cites is Gilroy, but the timing, the insulting hubris, and the involvement of Welles all fit the pattern set in Gilroy's statements. Welles meets the producer in the hope of playing Wolfe, a character he wants to portray after reading the Stout stories. The producer proceeds to call one of America's most admired actors by his first name, "Orson." This does not please Welles, who is meeting this producer for the first time. To compound the transgression, the producer informs Welles that the aim of the project is to make Wolfe "more human . . . more accessible to the American public." Welles's response is classic: "Making Nero Wolfe human is a little bit like asking Don Juan to have a soft prick." Welles gets up and leaves. The producer is left with his Nero Wolfe project, sans Orson Welles.*

Gilroy writes and makes the film. It sits in a film can on a shelf at Paramount. It doesn't make it to the television screen, nor is it programmed into a network schedule. In July 1978, a bit more than a year after it is completed, Thayer David dies. The film is still not aired. Finally, in December 1979 at midnight, the film is shown on ABC. After a load of money spent and the talents of Gilroy and others used, the film is described by a television executive as "not very good," with all due regard for

Gilroy's comment about the judgment of the Nero Wolfe literary society.

The television executive is right. It is barely passable if you're a Wolfe devotee, and only because it does contain threads from the book. The characters are weak, poorly crafted, or plain wrong. Archie is a smirking juvenile. Wolfe speaks in aphorisms that become steadily more turgid through the story, and he isn't even fat, though he has a jumbo head and full lips. He laughs a lot and expresses his romantic feelings for Mrs. Bruner. Mrs. Bruner is well acted by Anne Baxter, who is elegantly spoken, charming, tough, and beautiful – more beautiful than Archie's description of Mrs. Bruner in the book, but Anne Baxter is glamorous in the best understated way.

Like some snake-oil salesman, Wolfe lays hands on Lon Cohen to convince him to cooperate. Inspector Cramer vacillates between shoving Goodwin forcefully into a chair and then acting as Wolfe's willing tool to catch the killer of Morris Althaus. Orrie Cather is a thug who mugs a woman (reminiscent of an event in the first Wolfe novel, *Fer-de-Lance*, when the characters are still in formation). Saul Panzer is an aged, runt street urchin, whose only functions are to drive Wolfe to the Hewitt estate and laugh while holding a pistol on two FBI agents. Fritz is a witling, allowing a fake glazier to plant a bug in the brownstone after being told explicitly to take care with the FBI lurking. Surely this is the gang of deplorables to whom candidate Hillary refers.

The film gets underway with a fizzle as Gilroy totally ditches one of the best openings in all the Wolfe stories, as quoted previously, instead going through a bland discussion between Wolfe and Archie in the greenhouse, with Theodore present, saying that Mrs. Bruner has arrived. Archie then practically sings and dances in the office to occupy her while she waits. Shameless. Just as egregiously, Gilroy has Mrs. Bruner questioning Archie about Wolfe's possible parentage by Sherlock Homes. Wolfe interrupts them, holding what looks like orchid blossoms on steroids, and protests any inquiry into his ancestry. Fritz, the soul of discretion, spies on Mrs. Bruner in the office through the peephole. Wolfe plays with his darts while talking with his client-to-be. This amounts to a prolonged irrelevancy, serving no purpose in advancing the story except as a not-so- intelligent method of establishing Wolfe's quirkiness that would be better achieved by following the book! (See *The Golden Spiders,* the pilot film for the A & E series, for a neat approach to introducing these characters to a first-time viewing audience, utilizing cues from the original work.) Had Gilroy studied the Wolfe stories, he would know the classic way in which Stout introduces Wolfe to a new audience in the first book, *Fer-de-Lance:* the first line of dialogue is Wolfe announcing, "Where's the beer?" In the words of Michael Bourne, "and thus we know Nero Wolfe, a man of immense character indeed."

If a viewer turns on the Gilroy film at a high volume and leaves the room, the opening scenes would be exactly like listening to a 1940s radio program. It sure isn't film. Add to this the nondiegetic music that is corn at its worst, especially of the romantic variety to signal Wolfe and Mrs. Bruner are inches away from an embrace and a French kiss. Yuck!

Gilroy does add a well-written original scene in a Finast supermarket. Archie eludes an FBI agent by turning a sales price sign for 9l cents upside down to read l6 and thus cause a shoppers' stampede that traps the agent. The scene is quick, funny, and in stride with the Archie character. It is original and a pity Gilroy doesn't, won't, or can't write more that are similar.

The film is chock-full of scenes, dialogue, and bits that try futilely to acquaint viewers with the characters' eccentricities, proving Gilroy was unprepared and unfamiliar with the original story and had no confidence that it would shine through on its own. Network television in that era is more akin to a department store than a boutique. Lowest common denominator. Something for everyone. Try the sale items and stay for the full-priced goods. The appeal is to a mass audience, one that mostly does not know Wolfe but might be attracted to watch. The attempt is to make Wolfe "more human" and "accessible," which is blind to the very qualities that make him enjoyable – his intellect, his appetites, his sense of personal integrity, his personality. Wolfe is a rare and special commodity (as A & E understood originally, before opting for *Dog, The Bounty Hunter*), and a select audience, though not necessarily Wolfe readers alone, is required to build viewership.

If you're a Nero Wolfe follower, you'll have to fight back your gag reflex when Mrs. Bruner, at an intimate dinner for two at the brownstone tells Wolfe, "I regret we didn't meet years ago," and Wolfe coos, "I have the experience and wisdom to cope with your charms." Such talk over food at Wolfe's table! Double yuck!

Gilroy's writing pretends to sophistication by having Wolfe recite recipes for dishes to be served to Lon Cohen and the Ten for Aristology, babbling "salt and pepper" with each one. The scenes Gilroy cribs from the book are all deflated by the lackluster, misguided writing. With the suspects gathered in Wolfe's office, Gilroy has the camera track the assembled as they turn their heads left, one at a time, and eye their neighbors suspiciously, a weather-beaten cinematic prop about as suspenseful as watching a can of peas fall to the floor. Staging like that dates back to the silent era. Rather than have Wragg march into the office to be startled and angered by the presence of Cramer already there, Gilroy has Cramer produced from behind a closed door like a rabbit pulled from a hat. It misses the effect that Wolfe is putting the two officers of the law off their guard so that he can dictate difficult terms to them both. In the plot-crucial hotel scene between Cramer and Archie, Gilroy leaves out the carton of milk – the peace offering and symbol of the complex relationship the inspector has with Goodwin. It is a sterling dramatic touch by Stout that Gilroy is incapable of either staging or understanding. Gilroy succeeds in putting his mark on the story, but it is a blemish.

No Wolfe story is primarily attractive because of its plot. Stout's plots range from clunky to quirky to just right, but they are not consistently stellar. A Wolfe story is about what happens along the way to resolving the situation at hand, especially what Wolfe and Goodwin are doing, how Inspector Cramer explodes in fury, what Fritz is cooking, what is being said, and how it is said. Terry Teachout employs the clever term "literary entertainments pure and simple." Where it is all going is less of interest than the getting there, what occurs, and the persons met on the way. The Gilroy film misses this completely. It concentrates on plot to the exclusion of character development and fit dialogue. Rex Stout's dialogues are like musical sketches, not elementary school grammar primers. They hum along at a proper pace and take the reader with them. Ignore the music and the stories lose their appeal.

Gilroy replots the discovery of the murder weapon, having Wolfe and Goodwin beard the killer in Althaus's apartment to prompt her to remove the gun from her home and try to throw it in the river. Wolfe sitting at the murder scene is out of character, in place of the original device of Archie breaking and entering the killer's home to discover and re-hide the gun, as we would expect Archie to do. Gilroy's lack of understanding of the characters has him writing a convoluted plot turn in place of Stout's natural writing. Though he drops a suggestion about the river, how does Wolfe know his confrontation will force Dacos to try to get rid of the gun permanently rather than re-hiding it somewhere close and convenient for the time being? Apparently, Orrie is following her everywhere on a sure bet.

The sum of all this is Thayer David's Wolfe, with his exaggerated pronunciation of words, stentorian voice, overly florid language, and posturing, is more of an unintended parody than a portrayal. Archie, lost in the overtness of David's featured turn, is a cipher in the storytelling.

Buy or sell this film? Sell it at a bargain basement closeout. It is tattered goods. Gilroy writes a run-of-the-mill television detective story, focusing on the Althaus murder and barely plotting the great charade with the FBI in Wolfe's office, the highlight of the book where its lead-up and denouement are deliciously told. Gilroy's other television creation, *Burke's Law,* is twice as engaging as this two-hour snore, most definitely because of the suave actor-light comedian-dancer-singer Gene Barry as Captain Amos Burke and the quirky stories, written by a bevy of writers, none of whom is Gilroy, but one of whom is the great Harlan Ellison (four of the first thirty-two episodes). Perhaps the affection of the Nero Wolfe literary society for Gilroy's *The Doorbell Rang*, as stated by Gilroy and confirmed by a member at the time of the film's release, is due more to the prevailing scarcity of Wolfe portrayals and the predilections of the group's members then, than to the quality of the performance. Gilroy, who by his confession hunts financing constantly to bankroll his independent films, may be earning a quick buck as hastily as possible. Though Gilroy in 1977 hints that the FBI is somehow to blame for his film not yet being broadcast, the idea doesn't hold water. Two years earlier, Senator Frank Church's investigations of abuses shine a damning spotlight on the FBI; two years later, what does the FBI have to fear from Gilroy's flaccid film? I do not blame Gilroy for being Gilroy; an old Scottish woman once advised me, "The only thing you can expect from a pig is a grunt."

The question stands: why rewrite a master storyteller? That is what ruins the first two motion picture attempts in the 1930s

(*Meet Nero Wolfe,* based on *Fer-de-Lance,* is a jot less faithful to its original story than the Gilroy film is to its), it is what is wrong with the 1959 television pilot with William Shatner as Archie, and it is the downfall of the Gilroy film. One doubts Paramount paid $1.5 million, in 1976 dollars, for a film to be first broadcast at midnight. Consider, Paramount made *The Godfather* full-length motion picture in the same era for $6 million. *The Subject Was Roses,* Gilroy's most famous work, speaks to unearthed psychological wounds. Gilroy's *Nero Wolfe* is just such an emotional scar.

In 2001 A & E begins airing *A Nero Wolfe Mystery* as a scheduled program dramatizing the Wolfe stories for television. It is, if not the first, one of a very few television series composed exclusively of story material translated directly from the original to the screen. Maury Chaykin stars as Wolfe and Timothy Hutton plays Archie the narrator, as well as producing and directing the first regular episode, "The Doorbell Rang."

This version studiously avoids the pitfalls of its predecessor. Hutton, who has an Academy Award as an actor, displays his formidable directing skills with steadfast attention to the book. Not just to the book as written (executive producer Michael Jaffe is the screenwriter), but to the spirit of the story, the tenor and rhythm of Stout's writing, and the individuality of the characters. There are no off-the-shelf bits of television business or stock detective story emoting allowed. The usual suspects of hack television writers (and their attendant litter) are not involved. The background music, for example, is the opposite of the dated drivel used in the Gilroy film: it has a jazz flavor and is used intelligently to underscore the plot elements instead of attempting to wring out the viewers' emotions. There are, alas, at least two minor missteps in this film. When Wolfe, Archie, and the 'Teers (freelance operatives Saul Panzer, played by Conrad Dunn, Fred Durkin by Fulvio Cecere, and Orrie Cather by Trent McMullen) are dining in Wolfe's kitchen, one of the comestibles is an obvious, commercially produced pressed ham from a deli or a grocery store, not a Fritz-prepared one, as would be expected. Next, I do not recall the New York Telephone Company ever employing red telephone booths on New York City streets (except in Chinatown), as depicted first about forty-five minutes into the film. Additionally, it's a puzzle as to why an early scene of Wolfe and Archie in the office is filmed in semidarkness. It only achieves a murky tone, unnecessary to convey the evening setting. Surely Wolfe pays his electric bill timely.

Employing a stock company of actors for supporting roles, Jaffe and Hutton bring out strong performances from a cast who obviously enjoy the work and the story. Debra Monk as Mrs. Bruner is less glamorous than Anne Baxter, but more naturally acted and closer to the character in the book. Wolfe doesn't want to hug or dine with her; in fact, Chaykin's Wolfe flinches as she approaches him in exuberance upon the completion of his work for her. Nice touch. As Special Agent in Charge Wragg, the striking, bald James Tolkan gives a unique turn as a character not explicitly fleshed out in the book, though more essential for telling the story properly on the screen. He is a believable FBI higher-up, full of self-righteousness, bureau loyalty, and useful lies.

Chaykin and Hutton nail their leads. They inhabit Wolfe and Goodwin and, in doing so, create their world around which all the others orbit securely. Bill Smitrovich fills Inspector Cramer's shoes with ease. He is tough and proud, and worldly wise. Give notice in the hotel meeting scene how Cramer and Archie interact, Cramer's facial expressions, and the care taken by costume designer Christopher Hargadon to shod Goodwin in snappy two-tones, and the policeman in sturdy black brogans (director Hutton includes their shoes in the shots). As Sarah

Dacos, Francie Swift is sultry and enticing without too much effort. Her mischievous eyes and painted, full red lips announce an inner naughtiness that plays to the villainous role. Colin Fox is Fritz, and Fritz is Colin Fox. (If there is any question about Fox's identification with the role of Fritz, be advised to watch the last scene of the *A Nero Wolfe Mystery* episode "Poison 'a la Carte," acted without words by Chaykin and Fox but through their eyes. The characters' shared humanity is poignant.)

When the three 'Teers plus Archie stand shoulder to shoulder pointing their pistols at the retreating FBI agents, their collective performance makes a mockery of the similar scene in the Gilroy film.** In point of fact, the entire depiction of the office charade on the FBI is so on target that it makes a forthright statement of quality and fidelity to the book. It is doubtful to think it could be done, from every aspect, any finer.

Retaining much of the book's narration and dialogue, especially between Wolfe and Archie, the film condenses a bit, moves words around a hair, and edits for pacing. Hutton, Jaffe, producer Susan Murdoch, and the production staff make a film that fits the required format of time, space, and imagination of television, but they don't butcher the source. The proper description of their effort is devoted. Everyone involved is well versed in the subject matter, reverent with the material, and it shows. The foundation is solid.

Novelist John le Carre' warns, "Having your book turned into a movie, is like seeing your oxen turned into bouillon cubes." If that is somewhat true, then it is a question of the strength of those ingredients in the recipe for the film. In *A Nero Wolfe Mystery,* "The Doorbell Rang," the resulting broth is both strong and rich.

The book and its two iterations on film in America (Italian television produced a version in 1969) can be sampled and compared side by side by side. *The Doorbell Rang* begins its literary life in a wave of anticipation and some debate. The Fred Cook expose' of the FBI's shady side sets a stage for Stout to compose a masterpiece of detective fiction. Stout claims he writes it not to attack the FBI but to tell a story of his creation's quest for a grail, the needed response of the public to a hidebound bureaucracy that cloaks itself in God, the flag, and the country. Two production efforts attempt to adapt the story for television. The first arrogantly ignores the responsibility of using the masterpiece with wisdom and due care. The second effort brings us into the masterpiece, re-creating with finesse many of the reader's mental images from the book and providing its audience with an all-too-fleeting almost two hours of unmatched Nero Wolfe viewing pleasure.

It is worth noting Rex Stout's alleged antipathy regarding the visual media. In a 1974 interview for the Chicago Tribune, he says:

> "Because I hate the goddamn [visual] medium. I haven't seen a movie in 30 years. There were these two Nero Wolfe pictures, one with Edward Arnold, the other with Walter Connolly, and they were both so awful I wouldn't have any more, tho (sic) the movie and TV people have made me I don't know how many offers. I hate the TV, too. I think the telling of stories in pictures is the worst invention of the 20th century. It's going to stultify and finally abolish the human imagination."

It is also worth noting that 1959's television show *Nero Wolfe,* "Count the Man Down" is negotiated by Stout's representative Fadiman Associates, with Stout's permission, and for which Stout receives payment. A profitable damnation for Stout. A reading of Stout's biography uncovers a number of incidents in his life in which he uses contrarian argumentation to refute the bare facts. It seems likely his approach in this can be described in the same manner as Churchill's: "He could out-argue anyone, even when he was wrong." Stout, like Wolfe, is a silver-tongued orator with a touch of the zealot, but a highly selective zealot.***

Sources:

Michael Bourne (editor), *Corsage: A Bouquet of Rex Stout and Nero Wolfe* (1977)

Fred J. Cook, *The FBI Nobody Knows* (1964)

Timothy D. Dickenson and Rhoda Koenig, "After 68 Books, Nero's Creator Is Still Going Strong," *Chicago Tribune* (July 28, 1974)

Frank D. Gilroy, *I Wake Up Screening* (1993)

Alva Johnston, "Alias Nero Wolfe – 1," *New Yorker* (July 16, 1949)

John le Carre', quoted at "Why Write Original Scripts, When Adapted Ones Earn More?," *Economist* (August 28, 2018)

John McAleer, *Rex Stout: A Majesty's Life* (2002)

William Manchester and Paul Reid, *The Last Lion: Winston Spencer Churchill Defender of the Realm, 1940 - 1965* (2012)

Lee Margulies, "Clues to Stout Mystery Revealed," *Los Angeles Times* (1979)

Tom Nolan, *Three Chords for Beauty's Sake: The Life of Artie Shaw* (2010)

Rex Stout, *The Doorbell Rang* (1965)

   Speech at Books and Authors Luncheon (1966)

Terry Teachout, "TT: Forty Years with Nero Wolfe," *About Last Night* (January 12, 2009)

J. Kenneth Van Dover, *At Wolfe's Door: The Nero Wolfe Novels of Rex Stout* (1991)

Burke's Law, ABC (1963 –1966)

Nero Wolfe, Paramount Television (1977)

The Golden Spiders, A & E (2000)

A Nero Wolfe Mystery, A & E

"The Doorbell Rang" (2001)

"Poison 'a la Carte" (2002)

*I attended the 2001 Black Orchid Banquet and noted Jaffe's speech.

**In the pilot film *The Golden Spiders*, actor Gerry Quigley plays Lon Cohen.

***For an example of Stout's selective zealotry, see his anti-German expressions in his service as American propagandist during World War II.

VI.
Looking for Golden Spiders

The Golden Spiders, published in 1953, is a thrilling read. It's not as twisty and dark as *Fer-de-Lance*, nor as economically written and plotted as *The Doorbell Rang*. It doesn't have a social conscience like *A Right to Die,* and it's not set far from the brownstone, as is *Too Many Cooks*. It isn't a great Wolfe story, but it is a decidedly good one.

In its unique opening, Wolfe badgers Fritz for not cooking squabs in sage leaves, as is Wolfe's custom. Wolfe then tries to shame Fritz by eating coddled eggs and toast to show how Fritz has reduced him to such a pass. Fritz in turn acquires a "mood," likened to a kicked puppy. Archie rubs Wolfe's nose in the cruelty toward Fritz by eating the squabs and antagonizing Wolfe with, "If the smell won't keep you from enjoying your eggs?" Archie answers the doorbell and invites young Pete Drossos to "consult" Wolfe on "a case" to rankle Wolfe some more. Wolfe returns the jab by detaining Archie from watching a billiards match, requesting he stay to witness Pete's recitation of events and listen to Wolfe lecture the boy on the ethics of earning a fee. Pete reports the strange doings of a female driver "with gold spiders for earrings." Wolfe's parry to Archie's ploy, listening to Pete seriously, doesn't ultimately succeed, and Archie attends the billiards match. Everyone except the boy acts the juvenile in spiteful glory. This is a first for all-around peevish behavior. This is all in literary service to demonstrate to the reader that the brownstone isn't always one happy family: Wolfe can be a royal pain in the rump, Archie plays with psychological fire, they are all poking each other in the eye, and everyone gets bruised. And a boy can act more maturely than some adults.

While this first scene is rather lighthearted and comical on its surface, Stout crosses over to tragedy, as Pete is murdered by a vengeful driver and his mother engages Wolfe to find the boy's killer for $3.98, Pete's savings from cleaning windshields at stoplights. Wolfe's response to Archie, "You brought him into this house," is volleyed by Archie with a slam, "It's your house, and you fed him cookies." The grumpy and put-out Wolfe (or is he just guarding his emotions?) warns Archie, "I hope to heaven this has taught you a lesson." No one is in a good humor.

Wolfe commits himself to pursuing the truth, and a killer, when a prospective client, Laura Fromm, is murdered in a fashion similar to Pete after handing Wolfe a $10,000 retainer check. Fromm is flushed out by the mundane device of a Wolfe-originated classified advertisement for the woman with the golden spider earrings. It makes one wonder how many people scour the classifieds looking to get hooked into a murder investigation, a device Stout employs more than once in the stories. Frankly, it's not very imaginative and, after a pause, none too believable. The repartee between Wolfe and Archie that is the spark for this idea, however, is worth the suspension of disbelief. Wolfe knows he has an obligation to Pete's memory, and Archie won't let him forget.

Yet another murder by auto ensues, and Wolfe's frustration shows. Stout spends seven pages on Wolfe telling Archie, Saul,

Fred, and Orrie what a hopeless case is at hand. In earlier stories, this Wolfe might spin into a relapse. He is neither genius nor artist in this scene as he solicits the suggestions for action by his associates: Saul's is worth following, Orrie is ready, and Fred isn't up to speed. Archie assumes an undertaker's garb to put in play a stratagem concocted by Wolfe of shaking up the suspects by pretending to offer to be bribed for what he knows. No one falls for it, though Stout uses a similar attempt at deception in 1960's "Poison 'a la Carte" with better results. In *The Golden Spiders,* Saul's infiltration of a corrupt immigration assistance organization (the more things change, the more they stay the same) produces the breakthrough, enabling Wolfe to uncover the criminal activity and nail the killer. Three days after exposing the "vermin" who took part in the crimes, Wolfe burns evidence in the case, with Archie as witness. Wolfe asks about Archie being an accessory to this, and Archie states, "I'd love to share a cell with you." They're finally acting as adults at the end of the story.

The Golden Spiders has the distinction of being dramatized on television by both the *Rex Stout's Nero Wolfe* series starring William Conrad and the Timothy Hutton series on A & E. This probably is due to the contemptible nature of the criminal scheme, the particularly sensational and ruthless murders – a child, a woman, and a crooked government agent all bashed by a car – and the confrontation with the illegal immigrant smuggling gang. This is not an armchair mystery, so it is ripe for visual presentation. It makes for exciting television if handled properly.

How do the two television films, separated by two decades, compare to the novel?

The 1981 episode "The Golden Spiders" is the premiere of the *Rex Stout's Nero Wolfe* series on NBC. There is no pilot for the series because it is rushed to air by NBC television bosses Brandon Tartikoff and Fred Silverman "to resuscitate [their] moribund prime-time TV schedule." William Conrad, of *Cannon* television fame, is the replacement Nero Wolfe, following the withdrawal of Orson Welles from the project and Thayer David's untimely death. It is unclear whether Welles takes his leave from this quickie version of Nero Wolfe or from the 1977 television film *The Doorbell Rang*, the forerunner of the series. The record points to Welles's earlier absence, from writer-director Frank Gilroy's statements. What is clear is that this series is thrown together in haste, although the set decoration appears meticulously done.* Conrad states, "We didn't expect to go as soon as we did; suddenly, they said, 'we don't want you on in six weeks . . . now, we want you on NEXT week.'"

Conrad says he is a Wolfe fan:

"I have been reading Nero Wolfe books since I was a kid, and I've always thought they were the most fun of any detective fiction I had ever read. I never thought I would ever play the role, and all of a sudden, somebody offered me the job and I said 'yes' without thinking."

The series in which he stars is described as "a traditional mystery in which the culprit is usually revealed to the television audience near the end." Conrad sees Wolfe as the "brightest and rudest" of fictional detectives, a position that is mitigated by Conrad's decision to "highlight the humor between these characters that live in the brownstone" and allow the audience to see Wolfe "has warmth." These missteps, emphasizing humor and warmth over understanding Stout's writing, result in the audience never rallying to the series. Latching on to "brightest and rudest" in retrospect is nearer the mark.

The opening scene (set in the contemporary early 1980s) is neutered into Wolfe throwing a fit about the squabs and cranky Fritz complaining loudly to Archie. The Archie needle of eating the squabs is lost. As is Archie going to a billiards match (he's now out to a date with "Dawn," giving Wolfe the trite rejoinder, "There'll always be another dawn"), and Wolfe serving Pete cookies and Coca-Cola (forget about the guest being a jewel) is also lost. Adding to this ungainly beginning, Wolfe is positively jovial – smiling, cracking puns, chuckling. He's not angry at all, maybe a touch put off his feed, like a horse. Moreover, Archie explicitly tells Wolfe he let Pete in to jab him for the way Fritz is treated. There is no subtlety, no undertone, no psychological interplay among the characters. This is pure television schlock, cooked by schlockmeisters, the common diet of the idiot box. (Schlockmeisters not only hack to death creative ideas, they then proceed to rearrange the pieces of the corpse.) Take great writing with layers of meaning and boil it down to steam. Here in this scene, all hope of a quality presentation going forward is lost.

It's a race to the bottom from that point. Archie conveniently witnesses the stricken Pete in the street, after the hit and run. Now that there is no more need for Pete, the television writers keep him alive to hype the pathos factor: "Will he live?" asks a distraught Wolfe. Drippy, melodramatic music pervades the entire episode. Wolfe observes presciently, "I think we may have seen the last of Laura Fromm," which begs the question, then why aren't you stopping her? Fromm is pushed out of a window, instead of being run over, eliminating the dramatic tension of three homicides involving the same vehicle. These changes weaken the overall story for no justifiable reason – two television writers flexing their creative muscles to rewrite a master.**

To Conrad's credit, although he chuckles a lot, he doesn't yell like Maury Chaykin does frequently in his later portrayal of Wolfe. The award for worst performance in the episode goes to Allan Miller as Inspector Cramer, though a timorous Saul Panzer acted by George Wyner is a close second. Miller's

Cramer has zero gravity, dreadfully overplaying a pretend-tough New York City homicide inspector speaking through his nose. It is awful what he does to Cramer's image, slightly worse than a pathetically shaking Saul Panzer, who is a contradiction to Stout's original character. Both Miller and Wyner are veteran TV character actors who turn up in numerous shows, from *Murder She Wrote* to *Soap* to *Quincy, M.E.*, numerous times.

Making viewing matters much more unpalatable, the schlockmeisters dismantle Stout's plot, substituting an "L.A. assassin," a car bombing that Archie miraculously survives by using "a wire" to start his car that is blown apart (must be one very long wire out of nowhere), and the attempted murder of Pete in his hospital bed that is foiled by sure-shot Goodwin in close quarters. These are among the most aged television tricks known to viewers, leaving them to wonder, "Haven't I seen all these before in *Mannix, Cannon, Simon & Simon, Starsky & Hutch, Cagney & Lacey,* and so on?" The answer is yes. No gimmick dies in television when it can be recycled until it becomes regurgitated pabulum. Television's unholy avarice is fed by reusing tired, lame ideas.

The beginning and the end of the story are nearly what Stout writes but just about everything in between is all wrong. This is what becomes of humor and warmth, though I suppose that to a baby a wet diaper is both warm and funny. Conrad's comment about the show, which lasted for thirteen weeks, is, "How the hell should I know what makes a hit TV series?" Perhaps not trying to reinvent some of the finest characters and their stories ever created. It must be noted that Conrad is an accomplished actor – none of the criticism of his portrayal of Wolfe is a criticism of his abilities, only a criticism of his take on the character. It is way off base.

Behold! An earnest attempt in the opposite direction. In 2000, A & E premieres *The Golden Spiders,* the successful pilot that initiates the 2001 series *A Nero Wolfe Mystery.* It isn't a word-by-word filming of Stout's book, but a loyal re-creation within the storytelling constraints of film. Screenwriter Lee Goldberg explains his enjoyment of being part of the *A Nero Wolfe Mystery* series (Emmy Award winning screenwriter Paul Monash writes *The Golden Spiders* pilot):

> "It was, to the best of my knowledge, the first TV series without a single original script – each and every episode was based on a Rex Stout novel, novella, or short story . . . The mandate from executive producers Michael Jaffe and Timothy Hutton (who also directed episodes) was to 'do the books,' even if that meant violating some of the hard-and-fast rules of screenwriting."

Jaffe advises that by adhering as close as possible to the original content, including Stout's language and time period, means "you have to create poetic distance [for the viewer] – otherwise there's no art in it." The viewer must be brought into the story with its unique elements intact.

Most importantly, J. Kenneth Van Dover observes, "The A & E series was able to adopt verbatim both the sharp exchanges between Wolfe and Archie, and as well Archie's narration in voiceover." By laying a foundation squarely on Stout's storytelling, *The Golden Spiders* succeeds where its predecessor fails.

The psychological bickering among Wolfe, Fritz, and Archie is re-created almost exactly from the book. Archie offers "Wolfe's childish performance with Fritz, it would do him some good to have another child to play with." The majority of plot pieces set forth by Stout are present – the billiards match, the characters behaving less than maturely, the hospitality to Pete, the subtlety, and down the line, the death of the boy. It works on a level of authenticity that establishes the connection with the viewer.

Unlike the 1981 version, this presentation, in a 1950s milieu, is narrated by Archie, taking the viewer on the journey with his insight and quips. The story is his to tell as both the play-by-play guy and the color commentator. Also on board here is Saul Panzer, not quivering in his shoes but in character as written, actively engaged in uncovering the illegal immigration scheme. This Saul Panzer is not a weak-kneed bystander but a fulcrum to move the story, as is a bold Inspector Cramer (acted by Bill Smitrovich), aided by a perfect rendition by R. D. Reid of Sergeant Stebbins (missing in action in the 1981 version).

Contrast Conrad's position on Wolfe with Maury Chaykin's:

"I think that's something that's appreciated by Nero Wolfe fans. If you become focused on the crime, I think you're kind of in the wrong place. It's more the enjoyment of the characters and their eccentricities, and the reality of those characters."

Don Dale remarks that there are "exquisite subtleties of the complex relationship between Wolfe and Goodwin" that the 2000 film gets right, and these subtleties are the antithesis of typical television writing, plotting, and staging. Watching this version of the story, the viewer is less aware that it is a television show and more conscious of the strata of interplay of the characters and the pleasure of the storytelling.

Not every turn and line of Stout's story makes it into the film. For example, Wolfe's lecture of Pete and Archie on the ethics of earning a fee works well in the book but takes too much time on the screen without adding anything to the cinematic story. No film can successfully move every story element onto the screen because there exist limits on story structure and timing in film that aren't present on the page.

Many critics respond to this television film with admiration and appreciation. John Leonard says, "Finally, A & E got [Wolfe] right." Terry Teachout praises Chaykin and Hutton, saying, "they understand that the Wolfe books are less mystery stories than domestic comedies, the continuing saga of two iron-willed codependents engaged in an endless game of one-upmanship." Canadian critic John Doyle calls the A & E series "an absolute delight."

There are voices in opposition to these views, though they are significantly outnumbered and overwhelmed. The *USA Today* critic calls the A & E production "thuddingly mediocre . . . chintzy and the books defy adaptation." Watch the opening scene of *The Golden Spiders* and catch the lavish set appointments by production designer Lindsey Hermer-Bell, as Wolfe walks from the elevator to the dining room. Nothing chintzy here. *** In terms of adaptability from book to screen, it is doable if the production believes in Rex Stout and follows the essence of his written words and the characters as meant to be. Another commentator faults "uneven performances and a sense that it's more witty and urbane than it really is." The viewing public feels differently: A & E's *The Golden Spiders* achieves the distinction of being "the fourth most-watched A & E original movie ever." Its viewer reception prompts A & E to air the *A Nero Wolfe Mystery* series on its full-time schedule. During the series' second season, *A Nero Wolfe Mystery* consistently scores viewer ratings higher than the A & E network on the whole.

It is the fidelity of the producers, writers, directors, designers, and actors to the true heart of Stout's work that elevates the 2000 version of *The Golden Spiders* decisively above the 1981 television film. Make no mistake, neither film replaces the experience of reading Stout's book, but they do add to the audience's enjoyment through the characterizations and story. The 2000 version does that better than its predecessor on the small screen. Watch both and give credit to the artists for what you find in their art, remembering the seminal artistry and genius of Rex Stout and the immortality of his creations.

Sources:

Robert Bianco, *USA Today* (April 12, 2002), quoted at "A Nero Wolfe Mystery Explained," everything.explained.today

Don Dale, *Style Weekly* (May 21, 2001), quoted at "A Nero Wolfe Mystery Explained," everything.explained.today

John Doyle, *Globe and Mail* (July 12, 2002), quoted at "A Nero Wolfe Mystery Explained," everything.explained.today

Lee Goldberg, "Writing Nero Wolfe," *Mystery Scene* (November 2002)

Michele Greppi, "Sleuths Super for A & E Record," *The Hollywood Reporter* (March 10, 2000)

Brian Gorman, "Series Revives Classic Gumshoe Style," *Winnipeg Free Press* (August 17, 2002)

David Kronke, *Daily News of Los Angeles* (April 22, 2001), "A Nero Wolfe Mystery Explained," everything.explained.today

John Leonard, "Super Nero," *New York* (April 16, 2001)

Rex Stout, *The Golden Spiders* (1953)

       "Poison 'a la Carte," *Three at Wolfe's Door* (1960)

Terry Teachout, "A Nero as Hero," *National Review* (August 12, 2001)

Charles Tranberg, *William Conrad: A Life & Career* (2018)

J. Kenneth Van Dover, *At Wolfe's Door: The Nero Wolfe Novels of Rex Stout* (1991)

Richard Valley (editor), "Nero Wolfe at the Door . . . and Out!," *Scarlet Street,* no. 46 (2002)

Rex Stout's Nero Wolfe, "The Golden Spiders," NBC (1981)

The Golden Spiders, A & E (2000)

*The series is nominated for an Emmy for Best Cinematography in 1981.

**The screenwriters are Peter Nasco and the late David Karp (a veteran writer of dozens of television scripts) using the nom de plume Wallace Ware.

***Executive producer Jaffe estimates the value of the sets at $800,000 when the series is cancelled by A & E in 2002.

VII.
Passing the Pen

The kiss of creative imagination is often given by a cruel muse, who tempts acclaimed artists to perform at ever higher standards that are inevitably unsustainable. Not every Rex Stout story is at the lofty levels of his best. Some are mundane, lack vivid characters, have muddled plots, and present Wolfe and Goodwin in cranky, sometimes lackluster moods. (For a taste of how Stout's writing can occasionally dip in quality, read 1939's *Red Threads*, as Inspector Cramer bores the reader to tears solving a case on his own, or the tiresome 1952 Wolfe novella "The Squirt and the Monkey.") All the stories are worth reading; many merit rereading; a number are as memorable as a great bottle of wine you desire years after that first taste, or a dazzling spring day you daydream about in winter. Rex Stout is both genius and human, capable of extraordinary grand slams with his talent and a handful of strikeouts. His superiority at storytelling is such that even his misses can be fascinating, if not sterling.

The superior lyrics of Stout's dialogue, characterizations, and descriptions often outshine the mechanics of his stories' plots. As a case in point, in 2007 writer Madeleine St. Just authors a biting criticism of Stout's last Wolfe novel, *A Family Affair*. When this last novel is published in 1975, it is clear Stout knows his mortal end is near, and, therefore, so is the original series of Wolfe books. *A Family Affair* masterfully admits the inevitable cessation of the original adventures and characters loved by readers. It is a coda to four decades of detective fiction excellence. Is the plotting a bit forced to achieve this? Yes. Airtight plotting is not Stout's forte. In 2007's review, St. Just declares, "Stout's last instalment is weak." She then proceeds to list five plot elements that she says mitigate against the believability of Orrie ever being presumed innocent from the outset. She judges *A Family Affair*, "overall a weak ending to the corpus, with the characters barely a shadow of their usual distinctive personalities." The point she misses is crucial to appreciating the body of the Wolfe stories: Stout is an artist, his words sing like prose that is poetic dialogue; his characters have lives that even in fiction, interest the reader because we enjoy hearing them speak. Orrie is always the weak link. He is destined to be the death of the adventures. He almost accomplishes this in *Death of a Doxy*. It is as if Stout holds the storyline of *A Family Affair* until Stout's last breath, to fulfill this destiny of Orrie's flawed soul. Stout's mastery in this regard is unmatched. He writes the human condition with honesty.

Nero Wolfe concludes "only an artist can read a man's soul." In *Fer-de-Lance*, Wolfe admonishes Archie

> "Must I again demonstrate that while it is permissible to request the scientist to lead you back over his footprints, a similar request of the artist is nonsense, since he, like the lark or the eagle, has made none? Do you need to be told again that I am an artist?"

This describes Wolfe's creator as well, if a bit egotistically. Stout is a consummate artist at telling stories that hold the reader's attention and entertain at the same moment. Without a Stout story at hand, the reader actually misses Wolfe and Goodwin; the attachment is engrossing, like beloved relatives who visit and then sadly and abruptly leave.

The series starts in the early 1930s with the anxieties of the Depression, the mounting threat of the European war, and the nascent hope of America's recovery marshaled by the newly elected President Franklin Roosevelt on the horizon (Roosevelt is inaugurated in March 1933; *Fer-de-Lance* is first published in October 1934 and is followed by *The League of Frightened Men* in August 1935). After more than a decade of writing and having published psychosexual novels, Stout turns to the pure story ("pure mysteries" in Robert Goldsborough's words), naturally written, in the environment of an expectant American audience hungry for tales of wrongs righted by logic and reason – a more stable world out of insecurity and chaos.

Into the 1940s, four Wolfe novels are produced, with Stout's creative energies focusing on his propaganda duties during the war, resulting in thirteen novellas in which his writing is stifled by the limited format and the constraints on character development, crackling dialogue, and detailed plot. The novellas are not among Stout's best work. Author Loren D. Estleman offers the perspective that

> ". . . a man of Wolfe's girth needs room to swing his elbows . . . I find the novella form half-developed at best, like an egg that Wolfe would judge under-poached . . . As it stands, it manages to be both flabby and gaunt."

America is keyed in on the war and its immediate aftermath. The novels, however, as if concentrating Stout's talent, are solid accomplishments: *The Silent Speaker*, *Too Many Women*, and the first two parts of the Zeck trilogy, *And Be a Villain* and *The Second Confession*. *The Silent Speaker* has Wolfe fighting corporate/government corruption, and the last two novels have him facing a corrupting archenemy.   Wolfe brings morally degraded individuals to justice in a flawed world, just as America is bringing the Axis gang to the bar of ultimate law and battling the scourge of communism worldwide. *The Second Confession* deals directly with the allegation of a major character as a communist.

The 1950s and '60s find Stout's creative output at its zenith, publishing nine novels and twenty-two novellas in the '50s and ten novels and six novellas in the '60s. America at that time is in a post-war boom with industry, the economy, and global prestige and power at record high levels. Counterbalancing that is the spread of Soviet communist aggression, the arms and space races, and the explosions of racial and social unrest across the United States. At the top of Stout's output of novels at the time are two of his best – *A Right to Die* and *The Doorbell Rang*, the most politically focused of his body of Wolfe stories – and the conclusion of the Zeck trilogy with *In the Best Families*.

Stout takes five years between his last novel of the '60s, *Death of a Dude*, and the next one, *Please Pass the Guilt*, then two years later for his last novel, *A Family Affair*. This latter novel, plus *Fer-de-Lance* and *The Doorbell Rang,* are arguably among Stout's very best.

When Stout dies in October 1975, he is a fixed landmark in both American literature and culture. Libertarian commentator L. Neil Smith summarizes, "over 30 years, Stout lays out a clear vision of civility our culture seems to have hopelessly lost today." In *Catholic World Report,* writer Thomas Doran observes in a more popular vein, "Many passages in the Nero Wolfe stories are gut-splitting funny."* Another writer, speaking about Stout's craftsmanship, says, "Stout's strongest feature as a writer is his superb dialogue . . . he knows how to make a really interesting tale unfold."

Death is the final editor, and Stout's dedicated readers suffer a deep void with the end of original stories from the master. With the blessing of the Stout estate, former *Chicago Tribune* and *Advertising Age* editor Robert Goldsborough picks up the pen, and in 1986 his novel *Murder in E Minor* is published to significant praise and approval, including winning the 1986 Nero Award from the Nero Wolfe literary society for "excellence in the mystery genre." Goldsborough comes to reinvigorating the Wolfe stories by the most decent of motives – he writes his as a gift to his mother, a Wolfe fan, in 1978. Eight years later it is published, and the overwhelming opinion of readers is the book is well written, engagingly plotted, and true to the mark in execution.

Goldsborough captures and transmits the characters' personalities through incisive descriptions, accurate dialogue, and references to events in Stout's original body of work. *Murder in E Minor* picks up two years after *A Family Affair* and Orrie's death, a decent and understandable period of reflection for Wolfe, Archie, et al. Goldsborough brings Wolfe out of self-imposed temporary withdrawal from the detection business by cleverly constructing characters from Wolfe's youth, and these characters – conductor Milan Stevens and former flame (how else to tag her?) Alexandra Adjari – form the basis for a murder plot, along with a cast of suspects and the ever-present Inspector Cramer, Sergeant Stebbins, attorney Nathaniel Parker, and major domo Fritz Brenner. Goldsborough's timing, not hurrying the developments but letting them occur naturally, is as close to Stout's best as can be hoped. Goldsborough gets it right, and he applies reason and a clue unintentionally supplied by Archie to knit it together with wit and thoughtfulness. Beyond being a spectacular re-creation, *Murder in E Minor* on its own two feet is a very good Nero Wolfe story. Goldsborough draws the story to its close with an admirably written response from Wolfe to Lon

Cohen's question if Wolfe is going back to the active practice of the art of detection. Wolfe responds, "I'm not sure how you would define active practice. I've always viewed investigative work as an integral part of my existence. And at the present time I have no plans to terminate my existence." Bravo Wolfe, bravo Goldsborough.

Goldsborough follows this book with *Death on Deadline* in 1987, building the story around Lon Cohen and the *Gazette*, a plot focus that is long overdue. It, too, is eminently readable, though it is prefaced by an unsigned writer (who obviously is John McAleer, as explained in an insert to the hardcover edition), who praises and questions Goldsborough's effort in *Murder in E Minor* in the same breath. McAleer adroitly pronounces, "One can fondle the same phrases and mannerisms just so many times. Bob Goldsborough realizes that. He confronts honestly and openly the limitations and protocols which Rex Stout set for Nero Wolfe's world, yet he sees to it that Wolfe and Archie achieve freedom and self-expression within these limitations."

Robert Goldsborough writes fourteen published Wolfe novels so far (the fifteenth, *Archie Goes Home*, debuts in 2020), taking a hiatus from 1994 to 2012. Perhaps he recognizes the stark truth of McAleer's warning about innovating amid the limitations of precedent and the audience's primed expectations. Writing professionally and successfully is difficult, sometimes undervalued work. Carrying forward a legacy the mass of Nero Wolfe is neither easy nor encouraging – all the Wolfe fans form a formidable gauntlet, through which the re-creator must emerge as least brutalized as possible. Every devoted reader is a scalpel-wielding critic. One of the significant miscalculations in this situation is readers' expectation of Goldsborough to produce a Rex Stout Nero Wolfe story rather than a Goldsborough one. In contrast, the sanctioned Nero Wolfe short stories are so inconsequential and dull as to be unreadable and not warrant in-depth analysis and criticism.

Goldsborough's return in 2012 with the retrospective novel *Archie Meets Nero Wolfe* is welcomed by many readers as a positive contribution to the body of Wolfe fiction, though some shrill voices object that his version of the beginning of the detecting relationship doesn't conform to clues in the stories by Stout. It is a matter of demonstrable fact that Stout left dozens of conflicting clues about Wolfe and company, scattered over forty-two years in more than seventy stories. Stout is well known for writing first-time-finished copy, seldom, if ever, concerning himself with trivialities of house numbers, places of birth, names, and more. Clearly and by his own admission, Stout doesn't regard such minutia as important to the storytelling. That some readers think differently says much more about themselves than about the stories they read and follow. One Wolfe fan writes an entire book to document, explain, and set straight all such inconsistencies, and along the way state some of his own shameful, obnoxious personal prejudices using Wolfe's voice. Nevertheless, the book's publication is approved by the Stout estate.**

Some of Goldsborough's novels are more enjoyable than others, akin to Stout's accumulated work. (Goldsborough's *The Battered Badge* in 2018 centers on Wolfe investigating dire circumstances surrounding Inspector Cramer, an inviting premise, but sections of dialogue by and between Archie and Lon Cohen ring hollow and awkward, detracting from the reader's overall enjoyment of the story.) Paraphrasing author Robert Cormier, the beautiful part of writing is that you don't have to get it right every time, unlike, say, brain surgery. Stout is a master storyteller. Goldsborough is a popular and accomplished author. Both writers bear the weight of agents, editors, publishers, readers, and critics pouring over their every word, buffeting them back and forth. It is unfair and unwise to make direct comparisons between the creator of Nero Wolfe and his continuator. There is no comparison, and Goldsborough is intelligent and respectful enough to understand that, because he doesn't contend to be Rex Stout. He is deservedly regarded and evaluated on his own terms. His work is read, fairly or not, in the light of what Stout's original writings inspire in their mutual audience. But they are two very different writers. That Goldsborough returns to the fray and writes more Wolfe stories is courageous.

I have criticized parts of Goldsborough's Wolfe efforts, yet I am grateful to him. He keeps alive in print a world, a tradition, to which I return.

"The heard voice perishes, but the written letter remains."*** This ancient Roman proverb instructs us that the writer's craft possesses an innate longevity, perhaps an indestructibility, that must be observed seriously and revered. The commitment to pick up the pen, to further a heritage that passes from one generation to the next, is not to be taken lightly. It must be honored appropriately by both writer and reader.

A writer's conception of success is quite different from that of other professionals. John Steinbeck's biographer, Jay Parini, quotes the following from the thirteenth chapter of Lao Tzu's *Tao Te Ching:*

"Success is as dangerous as failure,

Hope is as hollow as fear.

What does it mean that success is a dangerous failure?

Whether you go up the ladder or down it,

Your position is shaky.

When you stand with your two feet on the ground,

You will always keep your balance."

Stout and Goldsborough are kissed by the muse. Stout's work is bestowed longevity and immortality. Goldsborough continues to labor in the vineyard, his efforts still being tried and considered critically by readers. Time will tell what ultimate fate holds for him on that ladder.

Sources:

David R. Anderson, *Rex Stout* (1984)

Michael Bourne interview with Rex Stout (July 18, 1973)

Ken Darby, *The Brownstone House of Nero Wolfe* (1983)

Michael Dirda, "Jacques Barzun . . . and Others," *American Scholar* (November 2, 2012)

Thomas M. Doran, "Puzzle-Plot Mysteries and Their Golden Age," *Catholic World Report* (May 10, 2013)

Loren D. Estleman, *Nearly Nero: The Adventures of Claudius Lyon, the Man Who Would Be Wolfe* (2017)

Mike Ghost, "Mike Ghost on Rex Stout," *Golden Age of Detection Wiki* (2006)

Robert Goldsborough, "Robert Goldsborough Discusses the Legacy of Nero Wolfe," www.mysteriouspress.com

>   *Murder in E Minor* (1986)

>   *Death on Deadline* (1987)

>   *Archie Meets Nero Wolfe* (2012)

>   *The Battered Badge* (2018)

John McAleer, *Rex Stout: A Majesty's Life* (2002)

O.E. McBride, *Stout Fellow: A Guide Through Nero Wolfe's World* (2003)

Jay Parini, *John Steinbeck* (1995)

Steven D. Price, *The Little Black Book of Writers' Wisdom* (2013)

L. Neil Smith, "'Intelligence Guided by Experience' A Brief Look at Rex Stout's Nero Wolfe," *Libertarian Enterprise,* no. 68 (March 31, 2000)

Madeleine St. Just, "In Defense of Orrie: a Nero Wolfe Review," madeleinestjust.livejournal.com (October 2, 2007)

Rex Stout, *Fer-de-Lance* (1934)

> *Red Threads* (1939)
>
> *The Silent Speaker* (1946)
>
> *The Second Confession* (1949)
>
> "The Squirt and the Monkey,*" Triple Jeopardy* (1952)
>
> *A Family Affair* (1975)

"Vox audita perit," thepassivevoice.com

*To appreciate how humorous Rex Stout's writing can be, read his article "Let's Take the Mystery Out of Cooking," in the August 1956 issue of *American Magazine.* He is clever, dry, and understated in telling his domestic cooking tales, both tall and comic: a joy to savor.

**Author Ken Darby voices a bigoted attack on homosexuals through the device of a letter from Wolfe in Egypt to Goodwin as part of the book. The demeaning and hateful diatribe is completely out of context in the storyline, attesting to its motivation as a deplorable screed by the author. The book is disgracefully sanctioned by the Stout estate who give their approval either without reading it carefully or by endorsing the obnoxious viewpoint carelessly.

*** "Vox audita perit, littera scripta manet."

VIII.
The Wolfe Works of
Two Contemporaries:
Alan Vanneman and Loren D. Estleman

The reader's fulfillment of all things Wolfe fortunately has many outlets. Beyond the films, radio programs, and television episodes, writers other than Robert Goldsborough have produced a number of pastiches and parodies to quench the thirst of readers of Wolfe's tales. A goodly portion of these entries are run of the mill, not very adept attempts at re-creation, or they are quirky for the sake of being quirky. The real accomplishment, of course, is not to merely put words in the characters' mouths; a select few re-creators breathe new life in Wolfe and Goodwin and their cohorts, bring light to newly discovered corners in their lives, and maintain traditions simultaneously with tilling new ground. Those writers who achieve this are a rare few. They possess the requisite knowledge and feel for the stories, and the imagination to make the new stories relevant and consequential.

Out of the crowd, the recent works of two writers stand apart. Alan Vanneman in 2008 publishes online *Three Bullets: A New Nero Wolfe Threesome*, that he labels "fan fiction." In

2017, Loren D. Estleman's *Nearly Nero: The Adventures of Claudius Lyon, the Man Who Would Be Wolfe* is published. Both men are accomplished writers: Vanneman is author of two Sherlock Holmes pastiches and several other books; Estleman is a National Book Award and Edgar Allan Poe nominee and the author of dozens of novels, including twenty-nine in his Amos Walker series.

They converge on Nero Wolfe from separate and distinct paths. Vanneman's narrator is the Archie Goodwin readers know and trust, the sly observer and legman prodding the reluctant Wolfe to detect. Estleman employs Arnie Woodbine, the highly suspect and not-smart-enough-by-half assistant to Wolfe imitator Claudius Lyon, to narrate a series of cases that are a comedic triumph. Approaching Rex Stout's creations from the right and left ventricle, Vanneman and Estleman penetrate the core of these characters and deliver carefully constructed, naturally paced stories, in due homage to the originals.

These two writers share a profound grasp of the uniqueness of Wolfe, Archie, the relationships, and the stories. They understand that these qualities are the drivers for readers, not the plots. In Vanneman's story "Invitation to a Shooting Party," Wolfe is seduced by a potential client's gift of a large venison sausage (putting aside the obvious Freudian imagery), to the point of putting Archie out of the house so that Wolfe may consume it by himself. Wolfe's overriding self-centeredness is alive and well. Fritz probably gets a taste in the kitchen. Estleman's Claudius Lyon is constantly catching his Arnie Woodbine in petty schemes to plunder Lyon's fortune. Though Wolfe still drinks beer, Lyon gulps cream soda, belching robustly in appreciation. Both sets of stories build captivating characters, but Estleman's genius is to do it in reverse! His foundation is ". . . hero-worshipping nebbish Claudius Lyon, shady leech Arnie Woodbine, and kosher chef Gus, sharing a Brooklyn townhouse with the tomato plants flourishing on the roof despite Lyon's botanical ineptitude."

It works. On every level, it works. The reader is drawn into the stories and recognizes the possible Mister Mxyzptlk nature of their existence: if they say their names backward, maybe they would turn into Wolfe, Archie, and the rest, but a few letters are missing. Each one is an achievement of Estleman's art to flip the serious/comic ratio and produce a great read. The mysteries, such as they are, are notches below the gravity of Stout's tales, but that makes them wonderfully digestible to the reader in these circumstances. The *Yiddishkeit* (cream soda, kosher food, Brooklyn location, Gus's accent) is on target. Many of Lyon's solutions are puns, misnomers, and groaners, to the advancement of the upside-down humor. They are worth every laugh as they fit the situations perfectly. Proof that the dearest form of comedy is born from well-told drama, the reader can't help appreciating the writer's skill in telling straight a funny story.

In "Invitation to a Shooting Party," Vanneman has Wolfe leave his home at Archie's prodding to solve the death of a wealthy woman, the gifter of the fresh venison sausage. I share the opinion of many other devotees that among my least favorite Wolfe stories are the ones in which he leaves the brownstone. His personality, more so than Archie's, is rooted in his home. That inextricable bond is meaningful; the brownstone expresses who he is and what he is about. In those stories in which he is interacting with the greater world for a prolonged period (*Too Many Cooks*, *The Black Mountain*, *In the Best Families*) the absence is understandable, if not preferred. When he leaves his abode to solve a case quickly ("The Next Witness," "The Cop-Killer"), there doesn't seem to be any good reason why he doesn't instead lean back in his chair, watch the bead settle in his pilsner glass, gaze at the globe, and put his superior faculties on the job. "Eeny Meeny Murder Mo" in 1962 is a novella, readable precisely because the story is tied to the brownstone, the site of the murder, just as Wolfe is tied to the instrument of murder, his necktie.

Vanneman takes a major part of his first story to set up the decision for Wolfe to decamp. It isn't complicated, but it is put together piece by piece. Yet it is satisfactory. Vanneman knows Archie's voice and how both Wolfe and Archie think and react to one another. Archie develops a female admirer, albeit a tad young, and Wolfe experiences the hospitality of an American country manor and diplomatic intrigue in the 1950s. For readers who would never picture him in a country-house murder case, he fits because Vanneman's touch makes him fit. The country-house murder case harks back to the early twentieth-century dichotomy between armchair sleuths and street detectives: Rex Stout is one of the first writers to bridge this chasm by making Wolfe Mr. Sedentary and Archie Mr. Action. Vanneman balances the two well. It is not beyond discussion that this setting isn't preferred over the brownstone, but it is apparent this one-time excursion does the reader some good, expanding the Wolfe universe in a different-than-usual direction. Perhaps *Some Buried Caesar* is a forerunner, though that early story is far more rough-and-tumble: the brownstone character is then not yet fully developed in the reader's mind.

Vanneman's remaining two bullets, "Fame Will Tell" and "Politics Is Murder" take place in modern New York. They are erudite and populated by true-to-form dialogue and characters. The latter story is a particular delight, with Wolfe receiving a $1 million fee, Fritz getting a new stove, Archie getting a memorable tip for his services, and one man's desires going unrequited. There is also a famous, some may say notorious client, whom Vanneman portrays with believability and ease. Of particular notice, Wolfe uses his logic and vast intellect to solve a thorny computer password clue. Vanneman's Archie is a burr under Wolfe's saddle in passages of him maneuvering his boss to get on the case. In both stories, the brownstone and deliciously described food are featured.

What are the expectations that either Vanneman or Estleman will go further down the path of book-length re-creations or reinventions of Wolfe and crew? Vanneman does post an excellent new short story in 2019, so hope springs eternal. For sure, it is a difficult task – just ask Robert Goldsborough. The creative pressure and challenge are probably sufficient for once in a writing career.

Estleman's work is a series of pastiches written from 2008 to 2016. *Nearly Nero* presents these and several more. The comedy contained therein may be too rich and enormously pleasurable for the reader to expect a second collected helping. The objective is to enjoy it now. While modesty may limit Vanneman to labeling his work "fan fiction," I am under no such constraint. It isn't – it has the depth and levels of detail and faithfulness that are far beyond the effort of a fanboy. To know of Wolfe is to savor him, but to write into the Wolfe world with seriousness to produce at a top level of quality is to write original fiction. Original Nero Wolfe fiction. Estleman and Vanneman both reach the mark, and we are better for it.

Will Vanneman one day pick up the pen officially? When the time comes to pass the pen next, Vanneman should be first in mind.

Sources:

Loren D. Estleman, *Nearly Nero: The Adventures of Claudius Lyon, the Man Who Would Be Wolfe* (2017)

Rex Stout, *Too Many Cooks* (1938)

    Some Buried Caesar (1939)

    In the Best Families (1950)

    "The Cop Killer," *Triple Jeopardy* (1952)

    The Black Mountain (1954)

    "The Next Witness," *Three Witnesses* (1956)

    "Eeny Meeny Murder Mo," *Homicide Trinity* (1962)

J. Kenneth Van Dover, *At Wolfe's Door: The Nero Wolfe Novels of Rex Stout* (1991)

Alan Vanneman, *Three Bullets: A New Nero Wolfe Threesome* (2008)

IX.
Review: *Death of an Art Collector* by Robert Goldsborough

Robert Goldsborough's fourteenth Nero Wolfe novel, *Death of an Art Collector,* takes place in New York City and is an account of Wolfe and Goodwin engaging in a murder investigation in a unique milieu – the art world. Previous Goldsborough-penned Wolfe novels revolve around the environments of the newspaper business (*Death on Deadline* and *Stop the Presses!*), advertising (*Fade to Black*), crooked politics (*Murder in the Ball Park*), and publishing (*The Missing Chapter*), to cite a few. In this respect, his works are similar to some of Stout's, who uses settings, among others, in the culinary world (*Too Many Cooks*), publishing (*Plot It Yourself*), advertising (*Before Midnight*), and animal husbandry (*Some Buried Caesar*). In these works, both Goldsborough and Stout exhibit a fair measure of working knowledge of the particular areas involved – Stout possesses proficiency in gourmet cooking, book production, the ad game, and farming and breeding from his own life experiences; Goldsborough is experienced in journalism, publishing, advertising, and the murky confines of Chicago politics. Hemingway advises "write what you know," and Goldsborough and Stout apparently emulate this advice to a certain degree, but not entirely.

Writing, truly interesting and entertaining writing, must go to the next level above just what one knows or what a character does for a living. Not just "what you know," but what you feel and sense, what your instinct determinedly tells you, and what you dream. Writers are bound to explore the human condition and its soul, to dig deeper than the characters' professions and material interests. To dig deeper within themselves. Remember Wolfe's admonition that only an artist can read a person's soul. Writing, according to John Steinbeck, is "a strange and mystical business."

Starting with his less than spellbinding psychosexual novels, but using their premises as the basis for many of his subsequent character portraits, Stout goes deep into that dark core of humanity and its flaws: the rage of son against father in *Fer-de-Lance;* the callous sexuality of Dina Laszio in *Too Many Cooks;* the unbridled libido of Thomas Yeager in *Too Many Clients;* the greed of the unethical lawyer in "Eeny Meeny Murder Mo." Stout writes the human heart with cold calculation.

Goldsborough's writing tends to not journey deeply into the psyche. Lloyd Morgan in Goldsborough's *Silver Spire*, for example, is a money-loving, sniveling coward of a killer, but he is too flat a character to compare in venality to the jealous husband, Austin Hough, in Stout's *Too Many Clients,* who beats his wife and coolly takes credit for it to Goodwin – and Hough is not even the killer, though he is sickeningly brutal. That honor goes to a corporate executive who kills to protect his company! Consistently, Stout's characters are insidious, iniquitous, nutty, and downright fascinating. Goldsborough tends to paint in the foreground and leave the background monochrome, though taking note that *The Battered Badge* does delve into Inspector

Cramer with some insight and include intriguing elements of subplot and backstory.

Goldsborough skirts the outer edges of the disturbed soul, but never seems to want to penetrate it in his Wolfe novels. He writes stories with suspense, but not Rex Stout stories. Cold calculation and examining the soul are not in Goldsborough's Wolfe territory.

And perhaps, that is just as well. Goldsborough writes Goldsborough, not Stout. To enjoy Goldsborough, the reader must accept him as a writer as he is. What Goldsborough does is to animate Wolfe and Goodwin, put into play the supporting characters, invoke the charms of the brownstone, and lay before the reader a tale of murder that is solved and resolved by the Great Pair. No confessions are beaten out of anybody. Readers are asking a lot, maybe too much, to bring Stout's entire incomparable style back to life; they may take satisfaction having Stout's created world back in regular print. Goldsborough writes, to quote F. Scott Fitzgerald, because "he has something to say." The real talent is to get readers to need to listen, again and again.

Death of an Art Collector begins with an early introduction of the cast of suspects, along with the soon-to-be victim, Arthur Wordell, the title's art collector. It is convenient to have them gathered together at one table, though not unbelievable. After all, what are acquaintances for, if not murder? (Wordell's estranged wife is introduced subsequently, but she is never a real suspect, and neither is his daughter.) Archie and his longtime female companion, Lily Rowan, are attending a preopening gala for the Guggenheim Museum in New York. Goldsborough tells the reader the story is set in the "late 1950s," a period in which Wolfe and Goodwin are remarkably active in detection, judging by Stout's output from that time.

Goldsborough's 2015 novel, *Archie in the Crosshairs*, also takes place in the '50s. Of his last six books, three are set in the 1950s, two in the 1970s, and one is of an indeterminate time period that is clearly after the 1940s. Two of the six, *Murder, Stage Left* and the current one, start with Archie and Lily attending an event that leads Archie and Wolfe into solving the crime soon at hand. With the exception of *Archie Meets Nero Wolfe*, Goldsborough's comeback novel after his eighteen-year hiatus, the succeeding six works have storylines that are either introduced by or directly involve one of the original Stout-created characters in Wolfe's world – Saul Panzer, Archie, Lon Cohen, Lily, Inspector Cramer and Sergeant Stebbins, and Lily again, in order. It can be extrapolated that Goldsborough the writer finds his comfort zone in the established Wolfean order and setting. By keeping the stories in the ever-distant past, the author doesn't have to account for and manage the inevitable changes and vicissitudes of the passage of time, events, and fashion. This may also be the path of least difficulty in attracting established readers to these new stories, as in "something borrowed . . . something old, something new." It is not necessarily negative criticism to observe that Goldsborough appears to be just fine in his happy writing place.

Victim-to-be Wordell is a starkly obvious target. Goldsborough draws him with clear lines as an extraordinary grump, with argumentative and hostile tendencies. Even without the book's title, the reader knows from page five, Wordell is going to get bumped off. He is an eccentric for eccentricity's sake, not traceable to some internal emotional conflict or wound. Eccentricities exist in stories for the purpose of revealing or explaining characters' fascinating personalities. Lacking this here leaves the reader asking, Why does Wordell rent an office in a dilapidated building when he can afford far better; is he hiding something or guarding a secret; why does he shun public discussion of his collection; why does he choose to befriend people in the art world, then pick vicious fights with them; why does he sit in the window with his legs dangling outside in open space? Understandably, the reader can feel that there is a lot more going on behind the scenes that is being withheld. None of these questions are answered in the story, leaving significant blanks for the reader. Regretfully, there is as much hollow space as there is substance.

Wordell's potential killers are offered with boldface motives that are plainly expressed. There isn't even a hint of a tease by the author as to what is going on in their minds. None harbor genuinely deep-set malice in the blood, matched next to, for example, Stout's killers in *Fer-de-Lance* and *A Right to Die*, for whom the reader must patiently wait to see them eventually tagged with the crime, and their hidden homicidal motives uncovered a logical piece at a time by Stout's Wolfe and Goodwin. Goldsborough's first five chapters don't dig up any surprises or deviate from his straightforward tale.

Accepting the author's style, and it is neither wholly unpleasant nor inarticulate, the reader may consider Goldsborough's story for its own features. Wolfe and Goodwin converse in intelligent and familiar banter, in neatly parsed conversations. The same describes Archie and Lily talking to each other, which occurs frequently in the first chapters. Wolfe drinks his beer from a stein now, rather than a pilsner glass. It seems Goldsborough is aware of the outcries from a number of readers of some of his preceding books about his excessive use of slang and colloquialisms, especially between Archie and Lon Cohen, because *Death of an Art Collector* is mercifully free of that. Goldsborough wisely relies on *The Nero Wolfe Cookbook* for the dishes described. Goldsborough is chided once before by McAleer for having Archie eat a pedestrian Italian dish in an earlier story. Archie is the narrator, though occasionally he is a mite too self-deprecating about his level of sophistication;

frankly, he's too mature now to try to hide behind the "aw shucks, I'm a country boy" routine. At this point in the characters' lives, Archie is with Wolfe almost twenty years; he's seen military service and handled plenty of tough guys and dolls. He isn't a rube or a shrinking violet, not that he ever was either one. He is around Wolfe much too long to not have a demonstrably robust vocabulary and wit, and not be proud of the same.

Goldsborough utilizes a number of the expected supporting cast (Inspector Cramer and Sergeant Stebbins, Cohen, and Fritz), but none play a pivotal role save Lily. He makes the editorial choice to tell and re-tell Lily's impressions of each of the suspects three times: once from Lily to Archie, then from Archie to Wolfe, and then from Lily directly to Wolfe after a Fritz-prepared dinner in the brownstone. Conceivably, this could be condensed without Wolfe having Lily to dinner, considering Archie's ability to report conversations verbatim. It is a puzzle as to what her face-to-face with Wolfe adds of significance. There are no concealed pasts or hoarded indiscretions revealed. Wasted words in a story are like Hamburger Helper in a dish – all stretch and no nutrition.

After passages of Wolfe's separate interviews with each suspect (mostly reiterating what Lily has reported twice) and brief visits with Inspector Cramer (who has little to do here), the reader is left with the same knowledge presented in the opening chapters. There is no burning clue, no white-hot motive for the murder. Wolfe is essentially stumped. On another day, Wolfe would call Saul Panzer and Fred Durkin for ideas and support. It is a mystery why he acts against the grain this time and doesn't ask for their assistance.

In the concluding chapters, Archie utters a number of foreshadowing comments, stating something awful is about to happen, leading the reader to anxious anticipation of a cataclysmic event, a bursting open of a clue, an uncovered motive, that spark of Wolfean logic that produces a memorable ending. (I, for one, could hear Carly Simon singing "it's making me wait, it's keeping me waiting" ringing in my ears as I read through to the climax.)

In Rex Stout's short story "Christmas Party," Wolfe, in an extraordinary personally compromising situation, declares forcefully, "I'm going to find the murderer and present him to Mr. Cramer." That Wolfe, the one the reader knows and admires, is intelligent, resourceful, and resilient. He is emboldened and is the master of logic.

That Wolfe isn't here in *Death of an Art Collector*. Here, Wolfe is bereft of his logic, resources, reasoning, and character. The killer, it turns out, could be and is just anybody. The story ends with a moan, not a shout, as Archie catches a brutal beating. This Wolfe is neutered and is the master of nothing.

Goldsborough, especially post his eighteen-year hiatus from re-creating Wolfe, doesn't routinely write nuanced, deep, psychologically challenged characters, with sinful pasts and unresolved animosities, in his Wolfe stories. (Milan Stevens and Alexandra Adjari, in Goldsborough's first Wolfe book, *Murder in E Minor,* do have those qualities, which add to that book's successful storytelling debut. The same can be said of Inspector Cramer in *The Battered Badge*.) They're generally not complex. He's not that writer of Wolfe.

Which is all the more a pity because Goldsborough's Snap Malek series from 2005 to 2017 contains plenty of psychos, oddballs, and troubled characters, with competently developed backstories and their own interesting lives, quirks, and features. Neo-Nazis Warren Jones and his sidekick, Becker, are not only demented anti-Semites, they're also overall bigots, thrill killers, and assassins in 2008's *A President in Peril*. Snap Malek's informer, Pickles, is delightfully strange and original, using hyper slang naturally in a way that is believable, unlike Goldsborough's slang overkill in *The Battered Badge* cited previously. The reader accepts Pickles in character, but not Archie and Lon out of character. Snap's mornings in the pressroom chats with his journalist peers ring true and convincing: they express their unique personalities and hold the reader's attention.

In *A President in Peril,* Goldsborough skillfully weaves into the story the character of automobile visionary Preston Tucker, elements of the game of Scrabble, and the circumstances of the 1948 presidential race. These are interlaced in the storytelling with a warm portrait of the protagonist's domestic life, his work as a Chicago police reporter, his leg-pulling with his journalist colleagues, his ritual back-and-forth with Chief of Detectives Fahey, and his connections in the seedy side of town. The last five chapters after the mystery is solved hold the reader's attention as resolutely as the preceding seventeen. Goldsborough produces an entertaining, engaging tale, full of texture and flavor. It's a satisfying meal for its audience and makes the reader hunger for more Snap Malek stories. The reader knows Snap's world, is comfortable visiting it, and cares about his adventures; Snap achieves personality. This should be the same aim of re-creating Wolfe's world and it demands dedicated reinforcement and focus to work. Unfortunately for the reader, *Death of an Art Collector* is short of that objective.

The reader of Wolfe stories rightfully feels entitled to expect a literary feast of caviar with all the trimmings. At times, the reader settles for a nicely prepared omelet Fritz style, instead. *Death of an Art Collector* is hard-boiled eggs and white toast, without salt and pepper. It's barely filling, but not nearly fulfilling. To quote Wolfe, "it's mere belly fodder." The stomach may be sated, but the real hunger, the craving, persists.

Sources:

Robert Goldsborough, *Death on Deadline* (1987)

    Fade to Black (1990)

    Silver Spire (1992)

    The Missing Chapter (1994)

    A President in Peril (2008)

    Archie Meets Nero Wolfe (2012)

    Murder in the Ball Park (2013)

    Archie in the Crosshairs (2015)

    Stop the Presses! (2016)

    Murder, Stage Left (2017)

    The Battered Badge (2018)

    Death of an Art Collector (2019)

Steven D. Price, *The Little Black Book of Writers' Wisdom* (2013)

Rex Stout, *Fer-de-Lance* (1934)

    Too Many Cooks (1938)

    Some Buried Caesar (1939)

    Before Midnight (1955)

    "Christmas Party," *And Four to Go* (1958)

    Plot It Yourself (1959)

    Too Many Clients (1960)

    "Eeny Meeny Murder Mo," *Homicide Trinity* (1962)

    A Right to Die (1964)

In memory of Charles A. Fish.

My thanks and gratitude to my editor, Jon Ford, whose insight and skill made this a better book. Any errors within are entirely my own.

There are a number of members of the Nero Wolfe literary society whose support and public encouragement are most valued. They know who they are. I thank them and hope they find some measure of pleasure in reading this one.

A special thanks to my fellow enthusiast, Bryan Hay, who, in his seventh decade, is still enjoying life's pleasures, most notably Nero Wolfe.